# THE GOD

# I SERVE

# CHAPTER 1

*Matthew 16:26 For what profit is it to a man if he gains the whole world and loses his own soul? Or what will a man give in exchange for his soul?*

It's a hot and humid ninety-seven degrees outside in Jacksonville Florida. Paul was standing on the corner of 45th and Moncrief on the phone while playing with the rocks in his left pocket. Paul is what's considered the normal now days, a drug dealing thug. He's 6'1 with an athletic build, very handsome and clean cut, pants sagging and has on a fresh new pair of Air Force One's. He sports all the latest styles and so does his women, which he prides himself on never being with the ghetto broads. She has to have a job and something going for herself. He likes them I-n-d-e-p-e-n-d-e-n-t! Paul, however, does not have a job but works nine to five every day, no days off. He's a slinger, a dealer, a street pharmacist if you will. Paul never was one to go through the ranks of someone else's operation, he just made his own. Wherever he went, he was packed down to the socks and always had the ammunition to keep firing even if his opponents stopped. He faced a lot of heat coming out of nowhere and taking over everywhere but he's smart and he knows how to run his business. Now all the dealers know and respect him, if they didn't, then they could expect to find themselves needing six strong men and a hearse.

Paul wasted no time asserting himself as the Don in these streets. There was a saying, "These streets are mean but Paul is meaner!" He was a nice guy, but only to those that were close. HIs glrlfrlend knew him as "Daddy" a nickname no one dared to even make fun of. Paul had grown so big that he was on the top ten list of every police and federal agency in 10 states. He didn't care. They couldn't stop him because no one would dare open their mouth. They knew that in order to get to one person, Paul would go through the 30 that stood in his way. He was ruthless and relentless but had a love for kids. He only wanted two at one time, but now he doesn't care how many because he figures he can pay for them all. He still hustles, no one knows why. The cops could bust him if they really wanted to, but why bother when most of the force is on his payroll...as usual! Besides, he loves his faithful, if you could call it love...

"Sup Paul"

Paul looks the young vagabond up and down in utter contempt and disgust.

"Sup Tim, where you been at?"

"Awe man you know, moms tryna you know, she uh tryna ummm...hey you got anything on you? I need something really bad right now man."

Paul laughs, Tim never did answer his question. Paul stares at him for a long minute. He watches how fidgety he is, watches how paranoid he is. He can see the sweat pouring down his brows. He remembers what this kid used to be, he remembers the day he got him high. Now look at him.

"What happened to you Tim? You had NFL dreams, million dollar goals, you were supposed to be quarterbacking our team, now look at you...what happened bruh?"

"Man Paul I still got a good arm bro...you should see me in action man. I can still take them wide receivers out...I just can't kick this thing long enough to get back out there man, but say you can help me. Paul, say you got something on you that can help this pain man?"

"You know what Tim, I got everything you need bruh...but I want you to understand, you ain't never gon kick this...this fa'life man. The best of 'em never get outta this and you...you're the worst of 'em partna! Now how much you got?"

"Paul man all I need is help and imma get outta this trap. I just need someone from the outside to unlock it."

"Negro what makes you think you betta than anybody else out here? What makes you think they would help you and leave everybody else?"

"I ain't saying that Paul." Tim realizes he hit a button; he looks at the scowl on Paul's face and decides to back down before something happens.

"Then what you saying negro?"

"I'm just saying I got enough for an eight ball!"

"Ohhhh Big Willie coming up in the world. Where you get the money for an eight ball cuz?"

"Man it don't matter where I get it from just as long as I can pay you right?"

"If I didn't know betta I would think you just got smart wit me cowboy!"

"Naw Paul, I don't want no trouble, I just want to get rid of this thirst man."

"Sound like you should be in that movie Blade bruh."

With that Paul reaches in his pocket and pulls out an eight ball. The exchange is made and Timothy is on his way. Paul watches him and almost wishes he wasn't his customer. Just as quick as the thought came, it left. He had a pocket of rocks to get rid of and in no time, he did.

Tim kept telling himself this is the last time. He lost all friends, with the exception of his junkie friends. He lost all the trust and love of his family. He stole so much and lied too much to the point that he really couldn't trust himself. He lives in any shelter that would accept him. He goes to abandoned buildings to get high so he doesn't get kicked out the shelters.

The thing about Tim is that he is a real hard worker and for that reason, people love him...but they fire him because he always steals to support his drug habit. He did whatever it took to get the drugs that his body depended so heavily on. He would steal a forklift with an alarm in broad daylight with fifty cops around it. Knowing full well he would never get away with it but these are the extremes he was willing to go to.

Tim grew up in a fairly large but decently provided for family. He had two sisters and two other brothers and they were all doing well. His mom was his biggest and only supporter. She would come lay hands, pray and read the bible to him. She would even find him in the abandoned buildings and pray for him there while he slept. She had to kick him out the house because somehow he would find his way into her locked bedroom and steal the mortgage money. She worked too long and too hard to allow him to jeopardize losing her home. She was the only one who raised the kids because like her son, her late husband had an addiction. He was an alcoholic though. He was functional, but if he didn't drink in the morning before going to work, he would be sick all day. He tried to get help, he even went to AA but that didn't do anything because the people in AA were drinking too.

He had no trust in the methods anybody used and that included drugs and hypnosis. He wasn't a violent drunk, but he couldn't do anything without drinking and it bothered Andrea, but she loved him and knew he loved her even more. He started drinking to help him forget the nightmares. He had so many nightmares. It was on one of these nights that he left the house and went to the bar. He drank a bottle and a half of vodka straight, and then decided to drive. Vodka and a speeding car on wet streets don't mix. He died at three a.m. from internal injuries he suffered from hitting a tree. Dang!

***Proverbs 10:2*** *Treasures of wickedness profit nothing: but righteousness delivereth from death.*

Paul sat on his couch looking at cribs on MTV. He loved that show, he remembered how he would look at the dope boys with the grills in their mouth, some gold but others had platinum and diamonds. He remembered the cars, the big houses and all the girls and parties. He remembered when he didn't have anything but a high momma. Now he should be on cribs. He got everything they got and then some. He sleeps with a different girl as many times as he can. He feels like this is the life. Paul kicks his feet up, leans back and relaxes. "Who can touch me?" he wonders to himself. Who can?

Paul gets a disturbing phone call. When he hangs up, the look on his face stops his girl for the moment from even thinking about asking him any questions. He grabs his keys and runs out the house in a blaze. He calls his boys to come get him. Something got to be handled!

Paul pulls up on 4$^{th}$ and main at 5:36pm. He sees Tim and knows what he wants, so he hops out the back seat and walks up to him.

"Waddup man, you ready fa'sommore?"

Timothy turns to catch Paul coming up to him with two guys behind him.

"Yea man, I'm I'm I'm ready man."

"What it's been two days cowboy? You hit that eight ball kinda hard huh cowboy?"

"It's been four days man but yeah, I need some more now," he said acting fidgety and paranoid again.

"Imma give you four rocks, fa' fifty."

"Come on man, dude down the street was gon give me eight rocks for the same price but I'm faithful to you man!"

"I'll give you ten rocks for free if you tell me where this dude is and what he looks like right now!"

"Come on Paul I don't wanna be caught up in the middle of nothing man."

"Negro if you don't tell me what I wanna know, its gon take more than these drugs to dull the pain imma put in ya, catch me?" Paul was in Tim's face now. He didn't seem to notice the stench coming from Tim as he stood there looking at him eye to eye. Tim had to take a step back to answer him. He had to because the two guys were now behind Paul and one had his hand on a chrome handle. There was no mistaking what message that was sending. He did what anybody with sense would do.

"He got on jeans and a white tee...long gold chain and he got a grill fulla gold too. He got shoulder length dreads, he bout the same height as you and he go by the name of Link."

"Link huh? Hmmm guess I betta pay Link a visit then."

Tim knew nothing good would come out of this. He watched Paul rub his hands together like something was up. He overheard a phone call he got while standing there talking to the two guys with him. This phone call seemed to have made the situation even worse.

"Oh yeah, you heard the same thing? Why the hell am I just hearing about it then? Oh yeah imma take care of this tonight...Link bout to learn a quick lesson on territories, trust son, it's done!" With that he turned back to Tim and gave him what he promised. Tim hustled out of there, quick fast and in a hurry. Paul watched him wondering if he would go tell Link but he knew Tim knew better. He knew what would happen if he opened his mouth.

# CHAPTER 2

*Romans 1:27* *Likewise also the men, leaving the natural use of the woman, burned in their lust for one another, men with men committing what is shameful, and receiving in themselves the penalty of their error which was due.*

"Travis you packed yet?" Travis' 6'4" frame tightens in anxiety. Nervousness makes his stomach do things it wasn't made to do. He feels his hands sweating and his mouth goes dry. Tyrone does not notice because Travis' back is to him. He's not sure if he's ready for what's being asked of him.

"Yo Travis, you deaf man?"

"Say what?" Travis turns around and plasters a false smile on his face trying not to show the tension his body is exuding.

"ARE YOU PACKED YET?" Tyrone raised his voice to get his point across since Travis acted like he didn't hear him the last time.

"Yeah, my wife's not too happy but yeah I'm packed."

"Travis what's wrong? You seem to be uneasy and uncomfortable. Tell me what's on your mind."

"Ty, are you sure about this? What if we're found out, what then? Is all this worth it?"

"Travis I'm not begging you to go, it actually might be a better idea if you stayed home. I don't want nobody all paranoid around me!"

"I'm not paranoid, I'm just saying..."

"What are you saying huh?" Tyrone rose from behind his desk and walked around it to stand face to face to Travis. His next words were important. They had to be calculated to give the right effect, all the training as a preacher had to pay off. He had to change his mind and set him at ease, Tyrone wanted him to go but his pride wouldn't let him say it so deceit was the next best thing.

"Look Trav...this is the trip of a lifetime. We're going to be ministering to the largest gathering you've ever seen. It's going to be good for you because you'll be able to see how ministry to this large of an arena really works. Nothing has to happen between me and you. I just want you to get your feet wet, that's all."

Tyrone's plan worked. Travis hung on every word that he spoke; especially the part about nothing happening between them. Travis was a sucker for anything Tyrone said, he was not only good looking but the man had power! They both had beautiful wives and children; matter of fact, Travis just had his first. His son was now 6 months old and was all he could think of when Tyrone wasn't intruding on his thoughts. Travis had dabbled for a while in homosexuality growing up. When he got saved, and especially when he got married, he assumed those feelings would just...disappear. Instead, those feelings came back even stronger because they were never dealt with, only covered up. Now Travis is struggling with being a father, a good committed husband, a God fearing man, and being an undercover brother in the church. He had a conscience, this weighed heavily on him. He knew he needed to be away from Tyrone but the attraction was so strong. He knew he couldn't do it by himself. The only other option, which was not really an option, was to tell someone. Who would he tell? His wife? An Elder? Or maybe even Bishop himself? All seemed unreasonable. He decided to handle things on his own.

"Well what time are we leaving?"

"We will pick you up around 6:30."

"6:30??? A.M? That early? Goodness man!"

"Come on man, ministry knows no time...so go home and get some sleep and let's do this thing man!"

With that Travis left. He still wasn't sure about the trip but if Tyrone said it was ministry then he was fine with that. Besides, he was excited about the chance to finally be doing ministry.

Tyrone smiled smugly to himself. Another one is about to bite the dust!

**Mark 13:33** *Take ye heed, watch and pray: for ye know not when the time is.*

Link looked at his watch...12 midnight. He's been out here all day, hustling; trying to get the last dollar before calling it a night. He still had a lot of customers flocking to him in the barely lit street. Maybe that's why he doesn't notice the totally blacked out Crown Vic across the street.

Paul sat in the back of the Crown Victoria eyeing the ongoing transactions with this wannabe nobody. He was very calm on the outside but he was seething with rage on the inside. He was the head of a multi-million dollar operation that someone was trying to hustle down. He wasn't about to let anybody see him sweat, especially over a young upstart trying to make his name. The problem wasn't that Link was trying to make his name, it was the fact that he was trying to make his name on territory that already belonged to someone else. That someone else happened to be someone extremely dangerous.

Paul watched Link pocket his money, his heart was full of contempt and murder. He caught a sight of the kid's face, he was young, very young, still a teenager kind of young. Paul made some phone calls to see who Link was dealing for, no one claimed him. He seemed to have come out of nowhere but he's been doing this for a while apparently. The business on this side of town was going down lately and nobody knew why. The crack heads were still there, the heroin addicts were still there, high as ever just not on his stuff.

He was still watching and waiting, waiting patiently for the opportunity to arise.  Paul didn't want to shoot his customers because he needed them to see what happens to anyone that tries to intrude on what Paul considers to be his!  His patience paid off, opportunity was about to knock.

Link had no idea someone was watching him, he didn't even notice the car parked across the street.  Once the last transaction was made, Link got on his cell and started walking back to his car.  He was smart he thought; he parked four blocks away so nobody would know what he drove.  He had a slow pimp swag that caused his chain to rock back and forth like a pendulum.  He was on the phone bragging so much about all the money and new clients he made today that he didn't notice the start of an engine and the slow roll of impending doom creeping up on him.

Paul sat in the back seat smiling, leaning to one side.  This is the moment he's been waiting for.  This kid is not much of a dealer because he didn't even notice his surroundings.  He didn't notice a car following him at all.  Something alerts Link, he notices a shadow moving behind him.  When link turns and looks, Paul's smile gets even bigger and he gives the order "Wet Him!"

Link sees the windows coming down on the Crown Vic, turns, drops his phone and tries to make a run for it.  Both the passenger's front and back windows come down and two AK-47's started blazing.  At first nothing hits the kid. He's ducking and dodging bullets whizzing by his head.  His heart is pumping fast; his vision is now tunneled.  His focus is on getting around the corner; he knows he has to pivot just right or risk giving those goons room to blow his head off.  How did he miss them? No time to think about it now,

14

the corner is coming up fast...he's got to hit it just right. Just as he's about to pivot, his back explodes in pain, then his leg and shoulder. He's out when the last bullet pierces his skull.

Paul looks at all the blood flowing from Link's head on the ground and smiles in satisfaction. Point made. The passenger gets out and rumbles through the kid's pocket and takes out all the contents. Paul signals for the driver to take off, he doesn't need to be found near any dead bodies. His message should be clear to anybody who even thinks about invading his turf again.

Link slips in and out of consciousness, fighting for life and breath on the cold concrete. He doesn't notice the police officer kneeled down beside him calling for an ambulance. The officer does the only thing he knows how to do. He prays.

There's so many things that he wants to say, I'm sorry, forgive me, help me, save me, don't let me die, but only the last words make it thru his lips "Please God."

The officer hears the boy and attempts to put him at ease.

"Take it easy son, you're gonna be ok. Just stay with me." The ambulance pulls up, the officer tries to move out of the way but a blood soaked hand grabs him. Link is afraid; he doesn't know what will happen to him now. Will he survive? Will he die? Is he paralyzed? The officer continues to pray knowing the young man is full of fear. He tries to assure him that he will be helped. Link's out again, this time no one knows if he will regain consciousness.

The ambulance pulls off, sirens blazing, with another young black man as its passenger. What is the reason for this senseless crime? The only evidence are AK-47 shells. The detectives are canvassing the area for witnesses, but none will be found. The neighborhood is run down and drug infested. This looks like a drug deal gone badly but only the victim knows, and he's unconscious with no guarantee of recovery.

*James 5:13-16 Is any among you afflicted? Let him pray. Is any merry? Let him sing psalms. (14) Is any sick among you? Let him call for the elders of the church; and let them pray over him, anointing him with oil in the name of the Lord: (15) And the prayer of faith shall save the sick, and the Lord shall raise him up; and if he have committed sins, they shall be forgiven him. (16) Confess your faults one to another, and pray one for another, that ye may be healed. The effectual fervent prayer of a righteous man availeth much.*

Tim sits on the second floor of his favorite abandoned house he uses to get high in. Another high had come and gone. He's been on a binge for three days. He heard what happened to Link and couldn't help feeling like he was somehow responsible for the fate of that young man. Link reminded Tim of himself, young and full of dreams. Both used drugs to get what they wanted. As Tim lights up his last rock, his head falls back as all his problems seem to fade. To him this is a place of Euphoria, a place of peace. This calm is what he hungers for; it's what his body craves.

Truth is sin is an unsatisfying hunger that no matter how much you feed it, though it may be temporarily satisfied, soon it will be not just hungry but ravishing.

"Hey man, hey, Tim ya hear me?" He waves his hand in front of Tim's face before rummaging through his pockets looking for more drugs.

"What are you doing?"

"Gimmie what you got or imma beat it out of you."

"Man I ain't got nothing else. I just used the last of what I had…leave me alone Teddy. Lemme enjoy this before it ends…"

Teddy, another drug addict, looks at Tim and decides to walk away. There's a few people that know Tim well enough to help him should something happen. He'll go harass someone else.

This is the price of being an addict. One is never safe. Through it all, Tim still knows there's a God and prays for His help. Will HE hear him?

Paul was back to business as usual. He didn't have any remorse over what happened to Link. He could care less. Paul knew the risks and understood the possibilities. He knew being one of the biggest drug dealers in the south wasn't going to be easy. He didn't lie to himself about that. He knew he had to always watch his back, his friend's and his girlfriend's. He knew every way to do dirt and stay clean. He knew the gangsters that shot Link were looking for a name. A name that meant no one would mistake them for punks. A name that would instill fear in the hearts of people when they thought of the mayhem these guys could bring. Paul was happy to oblige, matter of fact, Paul loved the idea.

Everyone thought that Paul had only a few options, but he had many aces up his sleeve. Paul knew eventually the word would get out because no one would keep this to themselves. They would brag and bring attention to the whole situation and Paul didn't trust them to just take the rap. Gangsters die every day! Paul had a plan and it would cause chaos and confusion but it wouldn't cost him anything.

Paul knew the kid didn't know who shot him. Maybe he should pay him a visit. Maybe he should darken his doorway. The idea appealed to Paul so much, he made it a point to find out the boy's name and room to do just as he planned; Sinister.

*1John 1:9* *If we confess our sins, he is faithful and just to forgive us our sins, and to cleanse us from all unrighteousness.*

As Travis sat on the veranda with the door to the room closed, tears flowed down his eyes. Tyrone lay in the bed behind him oblivious to what was going on. Travis was so caught up in condemnation that he couldn't feel the sharp drop in the temperature outside. He sat there with nothing but his pajama pants on begging and pleading with God for forgiveness. He thought this was what he needed, what his wife couldn't give him. He never thought about what would happen after the deed, and that is what the devil was banking on. When he got what he thought he wanted, all he could do was shake his head, then slump in the chair. He felt ashamed, dirty, unworthy and unfit for the duty ahead of him. What could he do now? Travis thought about his wife, his child and his life as he knew it, and became afraid. He was afraid of the possibility that this one act destroyed what it took him so long to build.

Travis couldn't sleep but Tyrone slept all night, even woke up praising God. Travis thought to himself that even hypocrites can offer praise, though it's not accepted. Tyrone did what he came to do, set the audience on fire and save some souls as well as pick up, pass and exchange a few demons. Who cares? The naked eyes cannot see this! Tyrone felt like he was doing the Lord's work when laying hands, preaching and teaching, doing all these things that

God commanded him to do. He doesn't think anything about those things that are not of God because he feels like he's human. He's allowed to make mistakes. After all, he's not Jesus!

# CHAPTER 3

Link wakes up; tubes are all over him and one down his throat. His head was bandaged and he couldn't see out of his left eye. He tried to move his head to see exactly where he was but his shoulder hurt so badly, all he could do was grimace. His back felt like fire was seething through every bone and muscle. He decided to just lay still maybe the pain would disappear. He didn't notice his mother in the background but she noticed him. She was careful as she approached his bed, she didn't want to startle him. She wanted to see his eyes but it hurt her to her heart to see her only child lying in this hospital in so much pain, with the uncertainty of whether he'll be able to walk again.

She couldn't help but cry as she touched his hand. He quickly grabbed hers. If that police didn't hear those gunshots, her child would be dead right now. She knew God spared him, for that she is thankful. She wanted to hold him so bad to ease his pain, but she couldn't help thinking, 'what was he doing over there? Why was he out there so late on a drug infested corner?' She speaks to him in a calm voice trying to make sure he doesn't panic.

*Proverbs 20:7* *The just man walketh in his integrity: his children are blessed after him.*

Officer Samuel Preston looks at the pictures in his police cruiser as he sits at a red light. He prays over the pictures of his children, something he has done every day since the day they were born. Never ceasing, he has to keep them covered in the blood. He does not allow one day to go by that he doesn't pray for them. He whole-heartedly believes that not only is it important but it is a vital link between man and God. Job sacrificed for his children and Sam decided to do the same. Sam knew God answered prayers, especially the persistent and consistent prayers of those that do right. When the light turned green, he pulled into the hospital-parking garage. He knew this kid was blessed by grace, but not covered in the blood. 'Did they pray over him? Did they anoint him with oil? Did they declare and decree that the Lord will lead his steps? Did they value him as a child of God or was he just another human to them? Were they even saved?' He took a deep breath and got out. It was something about this kid that affected him deeply. He always tried as time permits to visit at risk youths like this one. His brothers in blue always told him he cared too much, but he didn't mind though, this was what God wanted him to do and he was going to do it. He got a lot of tips from callers about this young man. He went by the name Link but his real name was Shawn McCloud, 18 years old and dealing drugs.

Sam knew the area Shawn was in was known to be Paul's territory. Paul, a name that was impossible to forget. This young man came out of nowhere to be one of the biggest drug dealers in the South. They will be investigating him later. As Officer Preston walked toward Shawn's room, his mother was exiting. He didn't know how she would react; after all, he didn't have any reason to be there other than genuine care. She seen him and the look of concern on his face and couldn't help herself. She broke down crying. Sam rushed over to her and before he knew what he was doing, he was holding her tightly as she sobbed deeply into his chest.

Karen was on her way down to the cafeteria to get something to eat and maybe a cup of coffee. This has been the longest two months she has ever experienced in her life. Today was the first day since Shawn got shot that he has opened his eyes. Karen was physically and mentally tired. You could see it in her face. She didn't want to leave his side but she knew if she was going to be there for him, she had to remain healthy herself. Sam joined her for lunch and they talked for what seemed like hours. She asked the hard questions and to his surprise, she listened to the hard answers. She had to, she needed the truth. She needed to know what her son was doing and how to prevent something like this from happening again.

Karen could tell Sam was a Christian; just by the way he spoke and carried himself. It wasn't fake at all, he was a man that spoke with wisdom from the past and a certainty of what lies ahead. What surprised her was the fact that he didn't mention God or Jesus or church, not even once. He was definitely different.

Sam was very observant; it was his job to notice even the smallest details. He watched Karen and knew he didn't want to push her away because she wasn't saved, but he also knew this was not the time nor opportunity to dig into her salvation either. Sam continued to listen as Karen talked and only asked questions when they were called for. In doing so, he learned she was a single mother and Shawn was her only child. She was the Director of Nursing at another hospital. Karen asked why God would spare her son, while so many others have died in situations that are not to be compared to her son's. Sam couldn't explain why God did some of the things HE did and neither did he try to explain.

Karen did everything she thought she had to do to make sure Shawn didn't grow up like she did. She worked two jobs to be able to provide him with the clothes that he liked to wear, while she wore anything. She made sure he went only to the best schools. Her intentions were well founded but she disregarded the spiritual things in exchange for the material. Her mother was a praying woman. She often wondered why she prayed so hard, because it didn't seem like it was doing her any good. Often times she would leave Shawn with her mother to go to the club or even just to hang out with her friends or boyfriends. She went through a devastating time when she got divorced and couldn't be the mother Shawn wanted or needed.

Sam wants to invite her to church but knows she's not yet open. It hurts him to know how badly she hurts and there's nothing he could do about it. Karen checks her watch and excuses herself to go back to Shawn. Sam gives her a card with his number on it and tells her to call him anytime. As officer Preston gets back into his cruiser the radio goes off. Domestic violence six blocks away from the hospital, duty calls. As he radio's in his location, he prays for protection, turns on his lights and sirens and hits the road.

*Proverbs 6:22* *When thou goest, it shall lead thee; when thou sleepest, it shall keep thee; and when thou awakest, it shall talk with thee.*

Andrea's hands shook as she tried to get dress. She had to sit and steady herself. No word yet from her youngest son; the athletic one, the one most likely to succeed. Colleges were scouting him while he was yet a freshman in high school. People were telling her how great he was going to be, how he was impressing coaches beyond college. She didn't know how true this was but she did know she was the epitome of a proud mother. She was expecting him to be drafted in the first round, expectations that were dashed during his senior year. She didn't know if it was the pressure to be the perfect quarterback that got to him and caused him to crack, or if it was the friends he ran with or maybe a combination of the two. It turned her once focused straight A student, with the pleasant demeanor and beautiful million dollar smile that made girls blush to their toes, into this desperate crack addicted vagabond whom she could barely recognize.

Andrea knew she was no perfect mother. She was once addicted to prescription pain medicine and smoked weed every day until the night Bruce died. Timothy reminded her of Bruce; tall, handsome, athletic and addicted. After Bruce, her husband of 22 years, died, Andrea yearned for something more, something that would fill the void that was left when he died. Her closest friend convinced her to try God. She did but it took her a long time to understand that trying God meant letting go of everything you thought you knew, and entrusting not only your life but the life of everything into his invisible hands.

Finally she's dressed. She takes a deep breath and heads out, in search of her child. She hasn't seen or heard from him in a month. She knows he's on one of his binges but never has he gone this long without contacting her. She's checked all of his known drug locations and nothing. She's gotten frantic wondering if something has happened to him, something fatal. She will go into the abandoned building that he usually gets high in. If he's not there then she will walk an additional six blocks to a shelter that he usually goes to. She brings him food, make sure he takes a bath and brush's his teeth, and if he's high, she'll lay hands and pray for him. The first building is blank, but someone gives her hope, they tell her he just left heading to the shelter. She thanks the stranger and heads to the shelter where she finds him.

Timothy watches his mother as she approaches him. He smiles but she doesn't. He knows she's upset. It's been a while since he's seen her. Her very presence makes him smile. She made him feel like life was worth living. He attempted suicide by overdosing a year ago thinking it would help and that she no longer needed to worry about him. That's not true, a mother never stops thinking or worrying about her child. She would rather come visit her son in a shelter than a cemetery. As soon as she seen him Andrea asked God to break this curse that has her child in its clutches.

"Hey Ma," Timothy stated, looking up at her with a Cheshire grin.

"Hay is for horse's boy! And where the hell have you been? I've been worried about you to the point my blood pressure is up. I don't understand why you do these things to me Timothy."

"Ma I'm sorry...what's in the bag?"

"I brought you some real good food, roast beef with carrots and potatoes, greens, dressing, potato salad and some good old fashioned banana pudding. I ain't trying to be prideful but I put my foot in this one."

"Ma you're the best thanks cuz I'm starving."

"You stink too. Go wash your hands before you eat one bite and while you're at it, here's a toothbrush and some tooth paste, brush your teeth too."

"You think of everything Ma, thanks."

As Tim rises to go take care of his hygiene, Andrea notices his physical changes.

"You've lost a lot of weight again Timothy. If you keep this up, I'm going to have to bury you in a match box!"

"Not that much Ma. It only looks bad cause my clothes is big."

"Timothy those clothes were fitting you properly when I brought them to you and that was only a month ago, so don't tell me your clothes are big."

"Yes Ma'am," with that Tim walks away to take care of his hygiene. When he comes back, he tears into the bag to get at the food. He was not sure of when the last time he ate or what he ate. She always packs a lot for this very reason.

Andrea watches her child with a smile on her face as he shovels her food into his mouth. She wonders if he even tastes it.

"Momma you uhh (chewing) you put both your feet and knees in this one! Thanks Ma, I appreciate it." He reaches across and kisses her on the cheek and then continues to devour his food.

"I know you do baby, go ahead and finish. I'll go get you something to drink."

"Coke Momma," he yelled at her in between chews. Andrea stood at the Coke machine contemplating whether to ask him to go back to rehab or not. "Dear God, help me," she prayed, as she walked back to him coke in hand. Timothy glanced over at her thru gulps and saw the look on her face. He knew she had something on her mind, he just didn't know what. And by the way she was looking; he didn't want to know either.

"Tim, how much longer must I see you like this? Must I die before you're free?"

"No Ma...you think I want to be like this? I hate being this way. It hurts you because I'm your child, but imagine what it feels like to be me. Imagine waking up every day with the desire to walk away, only to realize you don't have the feet to do so!"

"Meaning you don't have the ability?" Andrea asked as she reached for his hand.

"Meaning the ability was taken from you. Going to rehab is a great idea. If it worked! It doesn't work for everybody Ma. Most of the people I've seen in the rehabs are back out on the streets doing drugs with me. How am I supposed to put my faith in rehab?"

"You don't put your faith in rehab. You put your faith in God!"

"How can I? Does HE even care? Does He hear me when I pray? If HE does, why doesn't HE answer?"

"You may not be able to hear Him because you're not listening to Him. You're listening to the lies those drugs are telling you, the lies those other addicts are telling you. But that's why He puts people in your life who does hear Him. Trust me; if He didn't hear you then the devil would've taken you out last year."

"Aight Ma, but I don't want to see no shrink. I don't want no more medication cause all that does is either make me sleep or want more medication. No thank you. I'm tired of seeing my mom looking in abandoned buildings for me. I'm tired of seeing you come into the shelters worried and tired cause you been out on these streets all day chasing me down. If you say God can set me free then He's gonna have to do it right now. I don't see no other way out."

Andrea's spirit jumped inside her. She tried to remain calm and composed. Her son was saying the things that she needed to hear but she wanted and needed to know that he was sincere.

"I've been asking you for five years to come to church. Now if you want God to do something, will you at least put forth the effort in to show him you're serious?"

"I thought He knows my heart?"

"Oh he does, he knows every intention of the heart son. So make sure your intention is to get off and stay off drugs, not to just get me off your back."

"That's not my intention Mom. I like having you on my back. You don't weigh that much," he smiled at her. She caught onto the joke and smiled back. She had to admit, he still had that beautiful smile and sense of humor.

29

"Even still, just like everything and everyone else, God requires a commitment."

"What kind?"

"The kind that you would give to your drugs"

"I don't want to be committed to drugs Mom"

"But you are; your whole life is committed to them. You're so committed that you've let everything that matters go. You don't even see the value in yourself. I don't want to know what you've done to get the next high but I know you've had to sacrifice to get it. I know you've had to lie, cheat, steal and probably more than that to get that next high. This is not even what God is asking for. But son, give Him the same chance that you've given to these rehabilitation clinics, the same chance you've given to these shrinks and other drug users. Most of all, give Him the same chance you give to those that sell you these drugs."

"You should do a commercial for God." She didn't smile at that one.

"I won't make you promise me that you will come. You already know where the church is at. Come when you're ready."

"You make it sound so easy. Like if I come then it'll all go away; I won't crave the drugs anymore, or I won't shake if it's been a few hours since my last hit. You make it sound like this really ain't no fight."

"Son, that's not what I'm saying at all. There is going to be a fight because the devil is not going to want to let you go. He will squeeze and squeeze and squeeze, but if you let God fight this battle then you're guaranteed the victory. You've been fighting this battle by yourself for so long. Have you not realized yet that you're on the losing end? Don't you see the devil is whooping your tail? Or do the drugs keep you blind to that fact as well? No, this process won't be easy, but the results are going to be worth the work."

"So what am I supposed to do now to start on this road to victory?"

"Your sarcasm definitely won't get you on that road. You think about what you want to do. Whenever you're ready to commit, like I said before, you know where the church is." Andrea gets up to leave; she turns to walk away but couldn't at least not without one more try. "I've been in your corner from the very beginning. I've been rooting you on. I've been your water boy, coach and assistant. To be honest with you, I'm tired of seeing you get beat down but you got to want to fight cause I can't fight this one for you." With that Andrea walked away. She hated seeing him like this, so ready to give up but she didn't believe he was going to stay that way. She has seen a glimpse of a fighter in him today. He wanted more; he was just lazy. She would keep encouraging him, but the next visit she would push harder.

*James 3:1 My brethren, be not many masters, knowing that we shall receive the greater condemnation.*

Travis has been doing his best to avoid Tyrone at all costs since that night. Something inside of Travis won't even let him serve in the position of Armor Bearer any longer. After all, the armor is now tainted. Travis feels a heavy conviction. He didn't just commit adultery against his wife he did even worse; the adultery was first committed against God before it manifested in the natural. All Travis could do was sit in his car and shake his head. In the Old Testament, he would've been stoned for such an abomination. Now the stoning is coming from the shame and torment.

The fact that he had to reveal the truth (or so much of it) to his wife and the fear of her leaving and taking his beautiful newborn son! Travis could only think of his son and how this would affect him. Did he just generationally curse his child? Did he just ruin his son's chances of growing up to be a conqueror? Or has he damned him to be conquered all of his life because of the fathers sins? Deuteronomy 5:9 says "You shall not bow down to them or worship them; for I, the LORD your God, am a jealous God, punishing the children for the sin of the parents to the third and fourth generation of those who hate me"

Travis lifted his head and looked at the church he was sitting in front of. It was a beautiful two-story edifice; made of brick on the outside and marble floors lining the foyer.

Purple carpet lined the sanctuary, a sign of royalty. He walked slowly, looking at the chairs on the pulpit; which seat the most distinguished guests and senior ministers in the church. Tyrone sat in the one closest to the pastor. How could he not know? Travis questioned in his head, how are you so powerful in the things of God and can discern witches and whore mongers and prostitutes and drug addicts but can't discern that a homosexual sits next to you in the pulpit??? Travis's stomach felt like it hit his foot and his heart hit the ground, when he finally looked up and saw Tyrone. He was standing there with his hands in his pocket, looking like a GQ model with the biggest grin on his face.

"Wow! The dead has arisen." Tyrone said, eyeing Travis.

"Hey Ty, how you doing?" Travis asked.

"What's with the formalities? How you doing?" Tyrone mocked "Wassup with you? Where you been at armor bearer?" he said playfully jabbing Travis in the arm.

"I been here, you know...just chilling," he flinched but smiled.

"Been where Travis? Why you acting all funny and stuff? What's really going on?" Just then Tyrone's phone goes off; he answers and walks back into his office while waving Travis to follow him. He's talking to Bishop as he takes a seat behind a large mahogany desk and tells Travis to sit down. Travis won't look at him directly. Instead, he looks around his office as if he's never been in there before. Tyrone's eyes are glued to Travis. He's watching him intently. He knows something is wrong, but what could it be? It never enters into his mind about what happened between the two of them. He feels no conviction nor thinks it's a problem. After all, he's but a man! Bishop finally hangs up. The two just sit there; one is looking around like a kid in a museum while the other is watching him.

"Alright Travis, I haven't seen you, and haven't heard from you. What's on your mind?" Tyrone is first to break the silence.

"Do you feel bad about what happened?" he questioned.

"Are you talking about when we went out of town?" Tyrone asked with a frown.

"Yes I am" Travis answered boldly despite the disapproving look from Tyrone.

"Oh, so that's what's bothering you? I Should've guessed. Look Travis, ain't nothing serious between me and you, heck ain't nothing much really happened then anyway. So if you feel that bad then nothing else has to happen again, that simple!" he said with a shrug of his shoulders.

"Ty, you don't feel any conviction that we kind of committed adultery? Wait, not kind of, we actually DID commit adultery! Doesn't it also bother you that we committed an abomination before God? I mean rightfully we should be dead!" Travis was almost pleading with him.

"Hold up priest." Tyrone was starting to get upset as he stuck his hand out in a stopping motion. "Don't come in here with that foolishness. As I remember it, I didn't force you to do anything. You did it because you wanted me. You feeling convicted? That's on you, but don't bring your guilt and try to share it with me. I don't want no part of it." Tyrone said sternly.

"I'm just saying Tyrone, It's not like we're out and about with our status. We're hiding this, this is a secret from everybody but hey I understand your point of view clearly." Travis said hesitantly.

"Make sure you do.  We're not going to have this conversation again." Tyrone said with one brow cocked up to show he meant it.

Travis was shocked.  This man was oblivious to everything that he was trying to tell him.  It seemed like this didn't bother him at all.  Travis questioned himself on how many times did Tyrone do this? He was deep in thought when he was interrupted.

"So since you feeling so convicted, you gonna tell your wife?" asked Tyrone.

"I've already spoken to my wife." Travis shot back.

"Did you tell her the whole truth that you been with a man and not just that you committed adultery?" he smiled knowingly.

"No I didn't tell her that, it wasn't necessary." Travis said as he squinted as if he could see the intent of these questions in Tyrone's heart.

"Oh so church boy, it's necessary for you to come in here and try to make me feel guilty and you won't tell your wife the complete truth?" Tyrone asked as he sat back and smiled at Travis.

"I didn't come here to make you feel guilty or convicted. That was not my intention at all." Travis was beginning to get upset.

"Good cause it didn't and would never work!  Why did you come here today Travis?  Since guilt wasn't your intention, what was?" Tyrone sat up, wanting to hear this explanation fully.

"My intention was to come here and tell you I can't be your armor bearer any longer. I came to apologize to you for what I've done to cause the both of us to fall into this sin. Understand this, I'm no longer the same person that was with you that night, I can't be."

 "Oh ok. That's fine; change is good as long as I'm not a part of YOUR change." He said as he pointed his finger at Travis.

"Tyrone, I didn't come to make you a part of what I'm doing. I came to tell you I couldn't continue doing what I'm doing. Trust me; I'm not trying to get anybody else to clean out their closet. But the God I serve wouldn't let me stay in mine."

"Oh so we serve a different God?"

"Ty don't make this about you. I never said that."

"Let me tell you something. It's me that HE uses, not you, I am HIS anointed, not you. Without me you wouldn't have gone to a tenth of the places you've been to or seen the things you have. I earned that money, they pay me to come and preach. I am the one that HE chose, not you. You just happen to be the one that I chose and you can be forgotten just as quickly as I noticed you!" He said now standing and leaning over the desk to emphasize his point.

"Tyrone, why are you making this about you?  This is something that I have to do for my family and me. I thought you were better than this. I honestly thought I could come and speak to you openly about this and you would understand." Travis said looking up at him.

"You thought I was better than what Travis, then you? I am! And I do understand. You and your sorry little family can go and serve your God and don't worry about us. I got me and mines!"

Travis was dumbfounded, how did he miss this side to this "powerful man of God"? He was a man of god alright, just not the God everybody was thinking. All Travis could do, was shake his head as he walked out. It's like he never knew the man. He wasn't sure whether he should feel angry at or sorry for the man but he knew for sure the devil had a kung fu grip on Tyrone. Travis couldn't do anything but sit in his car and think about what just transpired. He thought about how the contempt seemed to leak from Tyrone like a broken faucet, how he so easily belittled him and his family, how he esteemed himself higher because of his gifts. Travis was able to now see why Tyrone wasn't convicted by their actions. He had demons galore! He understood finally that the devil don't mind you doing the work of God, just as long as you're doing his as well. Finally he drove off, not realizing eyes were watching him the whole time. Tyrone retrieved his phone from his pocket and called his wife. He told her that Travis has cheated on his wife and not to talk to her because he didn't want her around those kinds of "spirits". As he hangs up, he grins to himself "Stupid rabbit, tricks are for kids. Boy," he utters to himself as he leaves the church for a rendezvous.

# CHAPTER 4

*Proverbs 12:19* *The lip of truth shall be established for ever: but a lying tongue is but for a moment.*

A single bulb hanging in the middle of the room lights the interrogation room. There's nothing in it but a long table and four chairs. Paul sits quietly at the head of the table, the two-way glass directly in front of him. He stares at it as he contemplates his answers. Two cops enter the room. One brings Paul a Newport light and a coke; the other has a menacing look about him. Paul suspects he's the bad cop and the one bearing presents is the good cop.

Cop 1: "Paul James II, 25 years old originally from Brooklyn NY. Your mother moved here when you were five following your dad who was a musician that died from a drug overdose when you were nine I believe."

"Actually my dad owned his own business and he moved here because he was given a big contract. Thought the only way to oversee such a job was to be where it was. He was a musician on the side; it was his hobby to play the bass guitar. And he died when I was seven of a heart attack contrary to popular belief."

Cop 1: "Is that what your mom told you?" he said with a grin.

"What exactly does my dad and where I come from have to do with why I'm here?" he doesn't play into the trap.

Cop 1: "Do you even know why you're here PJ?"

"Umm PJ was my dad. I'm just Paul and no I don't"

Cop 2: "Paul, do you remember a young man getting shot, in what's deemed as your territory, three days ago; off of 45th and Moncrief?"

"Last time I checked, I don't have any business's running on that block. So no, I don't know what you are talking about."

Cop 2: "Paul, tell me where you were at around 11:45 and 12:15 the night in question?"

"Am I a suspect? Has someone seen me pull a trigger?"

Cop 1: "Just answer the question PJ. You don't have the authority to ask questions in here."

"Dang, I gotta wear a badge to ask a question, well guess what? Ask my lawyer where I was."

Cop 1: "This punk is lawyering up. That's what the guilty usually do." He's trying to bait Paul but it is not working. Paul sits back and crosses his arms in front of him, a show of defiance. Before Cop 2 can chime in and say a word, a knock comes at the door. They both exit the room only to find the chief and some unknown suit in the hallway.

Cop 2: "Wassup chief?"

"Gentlemen, this is Paul James's lawyer, Frank Mason"

"Officers, you arrested my client and brought him here on what charge? "

Cop 2: "He didn't get arrested. We just brought him here for interrogation."

"On what grounds?" Frank demanded.

Cop 1: "On the grounds of attempted murder!" he yelled.

"So in other words, you have no proof, no witness's, no weapons, no videos, no pictures which means pretty much you don't have any evidence. You're just trying to poke around until someone just confesses to doing the crime in question. Well gentlemen, with that being said, my client is not staying here any longer. And no, he's not going to confess to a crime he didn't commit. You have wrongfully held my client here, and you haven't advised him of his rights."

Cop 1: "Hold on Perry Ellis, why would we have read him his rights, he was not under arrest? We didn't wrongfully hold him. We told him we just wanted to question him about the attempted murder. Furthermore, don't come in here and tell me how to do my job!" The officer was heated by now.

"Actually this is a Perry Ellis suit, good eyes. Now as far as your job goes, come near my client again without a warrant and you won't HAVE a job!"

Before the cop could say anything else, the chief raises his hand to signal that's enough. Frank opens the interrogation room and advises Paul that he can leave now. Paul gets out of the room quickly.

As Frank follows, the cop has one more thing to say.

Cop 2: "How do you sleep at night knowing you keep murderers on the streets?"

Frank expected to hear something else. He knew the type of cop this guy was, hard nose and itching for a fight. Frank didn't think of what he would say next. He knew if he got someone mad enough, they would lose focus and make mistakes. Why not strike at his pride then?

"I sleep better than the boys in blue who commit murders and are still on the streets, to protect and serve." Frank laughed as he walked away. He struck not only a nerve but gold as well. The cop exploded in such a fury that it took four other cops including his chief to hold him back. That comment hit a raw nerve, since the police have been involved in several homicides in the past two months. Some of those cops are facing jail time.

Paul wanted to know what he said that made the cop start screaming the way he did. But Frank just advised him to keep low for a while and stay out the streets till the heat dies down a little. Paul usually listened to his lawyer and he will this time as well. The only thoughts that were going through his mind were that the kid still lives and somebody has been running their mouth. He's not worried about the kid. That kid has no idea what hit him, but snitches is something that he can't stand and must be dealt with. To Paul, being a snitch didn't just mean running your mouth to the cops; it also meant running your mouth period. Paul couldn't afford that. This was something that had to be dealt with and quickly.

*Psalms 91:1* *He that dwelleth in the secret place of the most High shall abide under the shadow of the Almighty.*

Andrea was all smiles as she crossed the street. She lived a few blocks away from the shelter so she always walked. It helped to keep her in shape. She knew Timothy wasn't out of the storm yet, matter of fact, it looked as if he was about to walk through one, a hurricane of a storm was coming. Andrea knew that no matter how big the storm, if she can only get Tim to trust God, he would see that yes, you have to go through, but HE'LL supply everything you need to make it through. She's praying as she walks, so she doesn't see the two characters coming up behind her fast. She felt a jarring hit to the back of her head. She knew something was wrong but she didn't know what. She saw the ground come up fast, as she put her hands out to dull the impact of the concrete. She didn't feel the pain. She just saw everything start to spin. She was being tossed around on the ground. She knew she felt hands but everything was happening so fast that she wasn't able to lock onto faces. She heard their voices as they searched her pockets, looking for money or anything valuable. They didn't find any. As they stood up in frustration, thinking what to do next, someone sees the gruesome twosome and yells at the two men hovering over her. They take off running as the pedestrian and friends chase them.

"Ms. Andrea, Ms. Andrea, Are you alright? Can you hear me? It's me Joseph? Ms. Andrea? Don't worry; I've called for an ambulance already."

Andrea knew the voice; it was one of the teens that go to the church. Joshua was a good young man, clean cut, who loves the Lord fully, and was neither ashamed nor afraid to show it. He looks around as he holds her hands. He's counting the minutes till the police but more importantly, the ambulance gets there. She finally gets her bearings and realizes something bad has happened to her. Her head is hurting and there's blood where she lays. Andrea tries to get up but is halted and comforted by Joshua.

"No Ms. Andrea, please don't move till the ambulance gets here. You might make something worse," he says with a look of panic in his eyes. She sees it and lays back down for his sake. He takes his jacket off and places it under her head so she didn't have to lie on that cold concrete. He was worried but he knew everything was going to be alright, she was a friend and the human thing to do is worry, but he knows who has the final say.

"What happened Joshua?" she asked, breathing shallow.

"You got robbed Ms. Andrea, but Mike and Chris chased those guys down."

"What happened Joshua?" she asked again.

"Ms. Andrea, I said you got robbed, did you hear me? Ms. Andrea?" Joshua was beginning to wish the ambulance had wings. He noticed her eyes were glazed and focused, they didn't move when he waved his hands directly in front of her face. He noticed a crowd was starting to form. As he asked a few of the people to move to give her breathing space, he heard the wail of the sirens coming fast. He leaned back down and patted her hand to assure her that he was right there and praying. This time she looked at him and smiled.

"What are you doing here Joshua? Why am I lying down? What's going on baby?"

"Ms. Andrea, you got robbed. You're outside on the street. The ambulance is pulling up now to get you to the hospital, you're going to be ok"

"Oh Jesus!" she exclaimed. She didn't know what was going on. One minute she was walking and now she's laying on the cold concrete with a crowd of people staring at her and blood running down her neck.

The ambulance pulls up but two police cars whiz by fast as possible. Joshua just stares, hoping they're going to pick up those two criminals that did this malicious act. The paramedics begin to question Joshua while helping Andrea. Another squad car comes with his sirens blaring, but shuts it off as he pulls up to the scene, BUT keeps his lights on. He gets out and Joshua recognizes him immediately as the officer from the church. He's friendly with Joshua as he asks him to relive what he saw happen. Joshua couldn't help but to hear over the police radio that the two men were apprehended six blocks away by two guys sitting on them. Joshua laughed to himself; Mike and Chris struck again.

Timothy was walking wondering how he was going to go through withdrawal again when he noticed a group of people gathering across the street. He was never the nosey type so he just thought to keep walking. Something, however, kept drawing his vision back across the street. He froze in his steps as he noticed the coat the officer had in his hand was his mother's coat. "It couldn't be," he whispered to himself. He ran across the street and told the officer who he was just as the paramedics was putting Andrea in the back of the ambulance. She told the medic to make sure her son is with her. Timothy jumped in the back of the ambulance to go with his mother.

Joshua agreed to go to the police station to give a statement about what happened just as Mike and Chris came up. They too agreed to go to the police station as well. They found Andreas ID on the robbers, as well as other articles from other robberies they've committed. They'll be going to jail for quite some time.

Timothy asks the nurse in the emergency room to call his older sister and brother. He loves them but they hate him, which is an understatement. Everything that goes wrong with the family, they try to blame it on him. He may need help but he doesn't deserve to be treated like a dog, even if he feels like one. He already knows what to expect, so he sits in the waiting room nervously awaiting their presence.

"Well, well, well the crack head still lives. Did you steal anything from the hospital yet?" They haven't even come fully into the room before they start ripping into him. Kevin is the second oldest behind Justine. They are one year apart, but mean as a pack of hungry piranhas.

"I can't believe you still putting Momma through this. This is all YOUR fault. It's cause of you that she's in this predicament. When she moves in with me, YOU will never be welcomed in my house. I don't even want you knowing where I live. I hate you that much. Why didn't you just die last year? I wouldn't have shed a tear at your pathetic funeral."

"Juss, I bet his own skin can't stand him, much less us. Why are you still here? What are you doing here anyway? Why don't you go get high somewhere? Disappear like you always do crack head."

"Did the crack take your hearing too cause you act like you didn't hear him say LEAVE!" Jessica yells at him just as the doctor comes in the waiting area to brief the family.

"Hey doc, how is she?" Kevin asked first.

"She's fine. She took a serious blow to the head. She's got a mild concussion but she's doing really well. We are going to keep her overnight just to keep an eye on her. We'll release her tomorrow depending how the next evaluation comes out."

"Can we see her?"

"Yes. She's a little groggy as we gave her something to relax her and calm her down, but yes, you can see her. Especially you young man," he points past Kevin and Justine to Timothy to both their disgust.

"She's been asking about you. If the three of you will follow me, I'll take you to her," the doctor instructs as he leads them to the room Andrea is in. She's all smiles when they walk in, which is usual. She has a tendency to make everyone smile. Andrea looks at her two oldest and rolls her eyes as they come in with scowls on their faces. She, however, is looking behind them for Timothy which takes an additional five minutes to enter into the room. She takes one look at his face and knows they had their way with him. Justine starts in with the questions.

"Momma, how are you?" she asks.

"I'm glad I got a hard head," Andrea said as she laughs.

"Momma, I see nothing funny about this. When are you going to stop allowing Timothy from getting you into situations like this?" she said as she pointed in Tim's direction "haven't you been through enough?"

"Listen here, ain't neither one of you the boss of me. This was some random act of violence. It happened, instead of complaining about your brother, why don't you thank God I'm still alive?"

"Cuz Momma, what's to thank God for when he's still going to be a crack head and get you into trouble? I mean leave him and let him die already Ma!"

"Kevin, you and Justine, get the hell up out my room. I didn't raise you to be hateful. I'm ashamed of you right now. You and all your education don't know crap! Go about your business. The only thing you two contribute is a whole bunch of evil. This is my son. I don't expect neither of you to understand anything but understand this; I'm not going to let either of you tell me what to do with my own flesh and blood. Good night!"

With that said, the doctor escorted the pair of piranhas out of her room. Timothy rose to leave but Andrea had other plans for him.

"Don't you go nowhere boy and don't pay them any attention. They're not me and they're not going to tell me what to do!"

Timothy finally looked up with tears in his eyes, "Ma, you wouldn't be laying here if you didn't come to see me. You wouldn't have gotten hit if you weren't on that street."

"Hold up boy, don't you start with that foolishness too. Now come here and sit next to me and let me explain some things to you," she patted the bed right beside her. He got up and wiped the tears streaming down his face and sat next to her.

"Now Timothy, the police told me that these guys were doing this kind of thing on the same street I live on, the same street I go to church on, and the same street as the grocery store that I shop in. This could have happened anywhere, you can't play into the lies that say it's your fault. It's not, that's crazy talk. Sometimes bad things happen to good people Timothy, and it's nobody's fault."

"Bad things seem to happen to you when I'm around."

"That's a lie straight from the pit of hell. Name one time something bad happened to me because of you?"

"The time we were at Uncle Ray's house and it caught on fire, because I was getting high in the basement and... well... you know what happened."

"Boy some things happen for a reason. You seen your Uncle Ray's house? It was a hot mess, he was a hoarder. I'm glad that happened; don't tell him I said that. All that stuff had to be burned and that house was condemned several times. He would just fix it and pile more junk in there that he thought he couldn't live without. Now look at him, he's in a brand new house. You can't get him to keep today's newspaper because he likes the clutter free look."

"But Grandma's sweater was destroyed."

"Boy, I hated that sweater! I just couldn't throw it away because it reminded everybody of grandma. I'm going to tell you something funny. Granny hated that sweater herself but granddad gave it to her. When he passed away, it was the only thing she kept that was from him because she knew she would never forget him, because it was so hideous!" This caused Tim to laugh hard. All of his beautiful white teeth were showing as Andrea watched him. She wondered how long it's been since he laughed like this. She smiled. They laughed for a while longer. None of the doctors or nurses asked him to leave. She talked to them about him all night. Andrea laid down and Timothy laid in her arms and fell straight to sleep. It's been a very long time since she's held her baby, even in this mess. Andrea has him all to herself, even if it's just for a moment. She's content.

*Matthew 26:52* *Then said Jesus unto him, Put up again thy sword into his place: for all they that take the sword shall perish with the sword.*

POP! POP! POP! The back windshield shatters, a bullet grazing the top of his right shoulder, a second through the front windshield, and a third in the passenger headrest. His heart is beating so hard, you can see the beats of his pulse in his jugular. He grips the steering wheel so hard his hand begins to hurt but he doesn't notice. His eyes are constantly moving back and forth from the rearview mirror to the road up ahead. Whoever just shot at him knows they missed, they're chasing him. He sees the car speeding up behind him. He blows through the stop signs and makes a quick right. He pulls his Ruger sr9c from his waistband, clicks off the safety, cocks the gun and places it back in his lap. The other car doesn't know what he's doing, they don't care. They got him on the run and they want to make sure he dies tonight! Blood is oozing from the wound on his shoulder but Paul stays focused, one wrong move and he's dead. Paul can't pay attention to the pain. He learned the hard way that pain is but a distraction that he can't afford. The car tries to pull to the side of Paul's bullet riddled Cadillac. He quickly slams on the brakes, jerks the old Caddy to the right, down a one way, and guns the gas. The other car, though newer, is not able to maneuver as fast but they're quick to catch up.

Pop pop pop, tata tat tata tata tat! There are two shooters now. Bullets fly past the old caddy, some hitting metal, some hitting the street, mailboxes, other cars but one gets lucky and tears through his right shoulder blade, comes through the front and lodges itself in the steering wheel. The pain surprises Paul. He sees double for a second and loses a half a second of breath before regaining control, but not before he gives away that he's been hit. His car swerves dangerously, hitting two parked cars and running over a curb before he pushes the distraction of pain to the back to focus on survival. He's already strategized in his mind what he's going to do. They know they've hit him. The smell of victory is close to their noses. The sound of sirens hit the air, so this has to end now. Paul smiles, they don't think and that's what he's going to use against them. He hasn't fired a shot yet because he has to be just right when he does. He knows he only has six bullets left and he can't waste them shooting at what he doesn't see.

They pull up beside him to end the rat race. Paul watches in his side view as they ease up to him. He doesn't turn his head completely but enough to see the passenger changing clips. Paul's hand was already on the piece sitting in his lap, but quicker than a reflex, he picked up the silver and black weapon with his left hand, stuck it out the window and shot three times into the car hitting the driver and passenger. The car veers viciously to the left, slams into two parked cars and flips onto its side. Paul smiles as he slows down, he knows he got them. As he comes to a stop in the middle of the road, he calls Frank to let him know what's going on. He leaves him a message. Police sirens close in as he stumbles out of his car. Lights blaring, guns drawn, all Paul could do was fall to the ground in pain. He knew he was alright but the pain told him otherwise. "Whoever did this is going to die, slowly and horribly," he whispers before losing consciousness.

"So what does it look like doctor? What do you think his chances are?" Karen inquires of the doctor concerning Shawn.

"Well his spine is still swollen, that's one of the reasons that he doesn't have feeling in his legs yet. Even when the swelling does go down, it's still not a definite that he'll be able to walk again. That bullet did a lot of damage, not to mention, the mess the other three bullets made. He's in pretty good shape considering what happened to him. We're going to schedule the second surgery on that leg as soon as possible. Also, we have an ophthalmologist coming to take a look at that eye.  His chances of survival are a lot better than when he first arrived."

"Thank you, I appreciate everything you and your staff are doing to keep my son alive."

"Oh we'll keep him alive. But when he leaves, you keep him out of here," with that the doctor pats her on the side of her shoulder and walks out.

Karen turns and looks at her only child, his eyes are on her. She's not sure as to how long he's been awake and listening.  She walks over to him smiling and trying to assure him that he's alright.    Tears  roll  down  young  Shawn McCloud's face.  Fear grips him, fear of not knowing what tomorrow holds.  Karen is trying to hold herself together to be able to keep him together.  It wasn't working too well. The nurse came in and gave Shawn some medication through his IV, he fell asleep pretty fast.  Karen sat down in the chair next to the bed, tears flowing steadily down her cheeks.  She put her hands in her purse to pull out a tissue and pulls out the officer's card.  She remembers him quite well.  He was very nice, truly caring, not like some people tell you they care but showed you different.  He actually showed a complete stranger that he really did care.  He just had a peace about him that she somehow envied.  She stared at his card for a long time then decides to give him a call.  The phone rings three times and just when she was about to hang up, he picks up on the fourth ring.  They talk for hours, she's asking and he's answering.  She inquires about the peace he has.  He tells her it's from knowing who he is and who he serves.  He invites her to find out for herself, she stutters wondering what his intentions are.  She looks at Shawn laying in the bed sleep and decides a little exterior air might feel real good right about now.  She agrees to go but advised him that she will meet him at the church.

Karen leaves the hospital feeling confident that Shawn will be all right without her for a few hours. She wanted to get something to eat, so she was going to ask officer Preston to go with her. Karen pulled up to the church at 7:15 pm. It looked kind of small like a storefront but it had a comforting feeling about it. People were going into the church, waving and smiling at her like they knew her. She would look around before she waved back just to make sure it was her they were waving at.

The atmosphere was very different around the church. She felt like all her walls and defenses were being melted away. Just then, Officer Preston pulled up in his squad car, jumps out and gives her the biggest smile that if the atmosphere didn't disarm her, his smile just did. He opens the door for her and they go inside. Karen didn't think about Shawn the entire time she was in Bible study. She had an amazing time and when they left, they went to get something to eat. She was very interested in coming back. She made sure to find out what time was Sunday service. Her and Samuel ate and talked for a few more hours. By the time she left, it was after midnight and decided instead of going back to the hospital, she was going to sleep in her own bed, but before sleep, she had to talk to HIM and they had a lot to talk about.

# CHAPTER 5

*1 Corinthians 6:18-19* Flee fornication…(19) What know ye not that your body is the temple of the Holy Ghost which is in you…

It's 7:56 pm and Michael is walking up the driveway. Sondra hears him on the phone but doesn't bother to stop what she's doing to listen. She loves Michael and wants to marry him but between him and her mother, marriage is out the question. Any time Sondra would bring up marriage to her mother, she would always ask, why she would want to mess up a good thing with a piece of paper. But she did want that piece of paper. She was tired of "shacking-up" as the older generation called it. She and Michael have been together for going on three years and living together for the past two. There was something wrong with the philosophy of "why buy the cow when you can get the milk for free" with her. She didn't share the same ideology Michael; she didn't want to be the free milk. But that's exactly what she's been giving Michael for the past two years, free milk!

When it came to talking about marriage to Michael, he would claim, oh one day they would do that. Soon they will take that step but he's just not ready yet. Even better, he wants to be sure it's the right thing to do. Sondra would always blow up in anger whenever she heard those excuses. She's good enough to live with and sleep with whenever he wants her, but not good enough to marry? They do everything as a couple, why not go ahead and make it official? Sondra had time to do a lot of thinking today due, in part, to her father. Her father is a Deacon at a small church downtown. He's pretty much the only stability she has in her life. He's a praying man, loves the Lord heavily and would do just about anything for her. She's been talking to him about her situation with Michael. He won't tell her what to do, but he lets her know everything she is doing is wrong in the sight of God. He tells her something that keeps her thinking all day. He says to her, "a woman ought to know her worth, cause if she doesn't, then a man can put any price on her!" She not only understood it, but she knew for a fact she didn't know her worth, because if she did, then she wouldn't be in the situation she's in with a man that doesn't love her like he says he does.

"Dang baby, I hope you thinking that hard about me."

Sondra just stared at him, she no longer seen him as the man she loved. Right now, she didn't know what she was looking at.

"Hey Michael, dinner is almost ready."

"Oh, I ain't eating. My bad, I ain't call you, but I'm hanging with my boys tonight. Tony is on his way to pick me up right now."

Sondra puts down the cooking spoon she was holding and this time she glares at Michael so hard it actually makes him uncomfortable.

"Why you looking at me like that? Didn't I just tell you I'm sorry for not calling you? I mean dang, you acting like my wife and stuff. That's why right there, why I don't want to be married."

"Why Michael? Because I didn't say anything? I just looked at you." She said matter-of-factly.

"Cause man, you think you own me or got rights to me like that. You just my ole lady, so stop acting like I owe you something Ma!"

"You're right Mike, you don't owe me anything."

"See you not wifey material right now." Michael said as he was pointing at her "You need to grow up and act like you want to marry me and that's real talk Ma."

"Preciate your real talk Mike. I'll take it into consideration."

"You tripping, I'm going to take a shower. I don't understand you. I'm with you every day and I can't spend some time with my boys?"

"I guess what's confusing me right now Mike, is the fact that I never said anything about you going anywhere with anyone. You're a grown man, do what you do. But while you out there, please realize, I'm grown too."

"Don't get your grown tail in trouble Sondra!" he yelled at her as he ran upstairs to get in the shower before Tony gets there. Sondra's mind is made up. She's had it, especially after talking to her father. She needed to really pay attention and get a grip on her own life. She wasn't going to say anything to Mike and she definitely wasn't going to speak to her mother about her decision. This was something she had to do for herself.

Sondra stayed downstairs and cleaned up the kitchen and put the food away while Michael was upstairs getting dressed. He must've been going somewhere nice because he came down dressed to impress and wearing his Polo black cologne that she gave him for his birthday. Sondra smiled, she knew he would be out there with all sorts of women, but this time, he was coming home to an empty house when he was done. Mike opened the door for Tony but didn't let him come in. He just barely got a chance to wave at her from the door, Sondra waved back. Tony was the nicest friend Michael had. Mike didn't even look at her; he just ran out the door and slammed it behind him.

Sondra finished cleaning up and was about to head upstairs when Michael came back in the house, he must've forgotten something.

"Look baby, I won't stay out too long, and when I get back home, we can spend some quality time together. I know you probably made some plans to hang with your girls, but bring your grown tail home tonight!" with that he kisses her and runs back out the door, hops in the car and they drive off.

Sondra is still standing on the steps, surprised that what he said didn't change her mind and neither did the kiss. It's like she felt nothing but…nothing. Sondra went upstairs and packed all her clothes and the rest of her belongings and called her dad. He told her if she wanted to start down the right road, then she could come back and live with him but Michael is not allowed at his house. Sondra agreed. She needed the structure and security that exists around her dad. She liked living with him, something her mother couldn't stand. She thought he was too overbearing, or so she claimed. The only thing Sondra remembers growing up is her mother always coming in at the break of dawn, sloppy drunk and watching her dad praying and carrying her off to bed. She said she left him, but Sondra knew better. Her dad got there in record time. He even carried all her stuff for her. He was elated to have his baby girl back under his roof, but he wanted to do things differently this time. He thought that maybe it was his fault that she left in the first place. She said it wasn't, but he knew had he taught his daughter how to value herself then she wouldn't let any man devalue her. He needed to show her how much she means to him and how much more she means to God!

Sondra felt like a kid, she was back with her daddy. On the ride back to the house, she snuggled up under him in the truck just like they used to do when she was a child. When they got to his house, and he showed her to her room, he blew her mind. He added on to the room a huge bathroom with a body sized tub, and bought her a brand new queen size bed and picked out the sheets, which was a dreaded pink color. She would sleep on it because daddy bought it. Once her stuff was in her room she laid back on her bed to think about all the things that happened today and ended up falling asleep. Daddy was there to cover her and turn out the lights but before he left, he kissed his baby girl on her forehead and smiled. They never do grow up, no matter how grown they think they are.

Paul wakes up dazed and confused. He sees lights but knows he's not dead because of the pain seizing his body. He doesn't remember much as he looks around the room trying to focus and figure out where he is. He tries to get up and manages to swing his feet out of the bed but had to change his mind and lay back down as his head starts to spin. He took a deep breath; he had to, because the pain was almost unbearable. The door opens and hears someone calling out orders. He recognizes the voice but had to squint to see him clearly. His doctor comes in the room, gives orders to the nurse and sends her away. Doc takes one look at Paul and smiles, at least he made it.

"You've seen better day's young man."

"Hey Doc, I should've known where I was but I was gone there for a minute."

"How you feeling?" He asks as he shines the light in Paul's eyes.

"My shoulder is blazing Doc."

"I'll give you something for that in a minute. Do you remember Friday night? I sincerely hope you do because there's some cops that have been here every day to see if you've regained consciousness or not."

"What day is it?"

"Sunday."

"Dang Doc, I been out that long?"

"You came in here after midnight Friday. So you've technically only been out for one day. So wassup Paul, what happened?"

"I went to TJ's house just to chill but wasn't feeling too good so I got in my car and headed home. When I pulled up to the stop sign that's when I felt the first bullet hit the top of my shoulder and bust out my back window. They chased me for a while, when they finally caught me, I fired three bullets. I don't remember after that."

"They brought all three in here, two died immediately but one survived until this morning. He's dead now as well. Paul, those three had the same tattoo as those two guys you got to hit that kid on 45th. Same tats Paul, you hear me, same tats, which means same gang." Doc whispered as he finished examining Paul.

"I hear you and know what it means Doc. I just gotta handle mines. These dudes need to be taught a lesson."

"Let your boys handle this. You need to rest and recover."

"My BOYS is who shot me! I don't trust nobody! So yeah, imma rest and recover as you call it, but not before I takes care of business. They don't know who I am, as if I didn't already prove myself. Well now I gots to do things my way, after all-Columbia is watching!"

"I'm not going to try to change your mind because I know there's no changing it. But Paul, do me a favor, keep yourself out of the path of bullets. They're unforgiving!" The nurse walks back in with a long needle and passes it to his old friend doc. Doc, as he's affectionately called by Paul grew up on the same streets but chose a different life. He never did let go of the streets though and Paul supplies all of his high society friends' habits. They stayed close, they took care of each other. It is a give and take relationship. Neither expects anything more or less out of the other. They knew to expect the simple fact that in this game, anything was bound to happen. Doc genuinely cared for Paul, he looked at him as a trooper, surviving where everybody else couldn't. He knew Paul wasn't a small time hustler but all that mattered was that Paul trusted him. He was there when they brought Paul's limp body into the ER, and he's going to be there when they bring his limp body into the morgue. That's just the way he thought, he wasn't dumb, he knew that by the way you live is the way you die.

He'd seen it so many times he became immune to it. He knew Paul would help him should he ever need it so he was going to cover for him as well.

"This is going to take you to lala land really fast. Sit back and enjoy the ride. By the time you wake up it'll be Monday morning and your lawyer will be in here to take you downtown to answer their questions. The thing that is helping you is people seen what was happening. Those guys weren't trying to be discreet at all. They were all out their windows shooting at you. People seen it and called the police."

"Thanks Doc, you're a lifesaver."

"It's what I do Paul, see ya!"

Doc didn't lie, that drug hit Paul so hard that he started slurring almost immediately. Paul saw two docs then none because his eyes were now shut. Doc stood there and watched the machines in front of him, Paul really didn't know how close he came to death but he wasn't going to tell him. Why would he, it's not like it would matter. His pager goes off, another trauma in the ER. He heads out and passes the two cops and yells out about him still being out as he ran past. He assured them he would call should Paul's condition change, probably tomorrow. With that he disappears, on to the next one.

"Tim, how you been doing with them drugs son?" interrupting thoughts that may not have been good for her youngest son.

"I can say I'm doing better but I wish I could say I was free...finally."

"I know you don't want to go to any more counselors or another drug meeting but..."

"But what Ma...But you want me to go back? Those people put me on drugs to take me off of drugs and the drugs they put me on; I would wind up being addicted to them too. So why not just leave me on crack or meth?"

"Would you please let me finish? That's not what I was going to say boy."

"I'm sorry Momma, please continue. I won't say a word till you're done." Timothy sits back in his chair and folds his arm in front of him. It was a signal that even though he is listening, he is already on the defense.

"Like I was saying before being interrupted," she smiled, trying to get him to let down his defenses, "I don't want you to go to those people. Instead, I would like for you to come to the church. We have a drug and alcohol ministry. It's not like what you're used to. No one is there preaching at you or condemning you. I've been going for a while, at first just to help out because the meetings get so crowded but then I started listening. What I heard made me wish you were there so many times. These are people who've been there whose helping people who are still there. Every addiction that you could imagine; not just to drugs and alcohol, but people with OCD's and sexual addictions are there. They are being helped in ways they didn't know was possible, or didn't think was possible, but they are being helped."

Timothy leans forward; a frown creases his forehead, as he looks his mother directly in her eyes. He sees her desires and knows that she wouldn't lie to him. She wants him to be free more than he wants to be free.

"You know Ma; I get tired of people saying you really don't want to be free. Cause if you did, you'd really be free by now. They don't know what this feels like. They don't know what it feels like to have your body control your mind. You think; 'I'm not going to do this today' but your body reacts in such a way that you have no real choice. The pain is so great. It feels like nothing you've ever felt before. I wanna be free and yea, I'll come with you. But what if it doesn't work" he asked worried from past experiences.

"It's going to work son because this isn't anything man is doing. This is straight from the power of God, and HE CAN'T fail!"

"When is it?"

"Tomorrow night at seven"

"Alright Ma, only cause it's you. "

"Baby Boy, I'm going to be with you every step of the way."

"Ma, you've been with me every step of the way this far. I don't doubt you'll be there for the rest but it's about to get ugly."

"I'm not sure what that means and really I don't care but yes, I will be there for the rest of the way. Jason brought over some of his old clothes for you. They don't fit his chunky butt anymore."

They both chuckled. Jason was another one of Tim's brothers.

"He gained weight again? How is he? I haven't seen him in a minute."

"He's good baby, secretive as usual, but I still pray that God do something in his life too."

"I'm going to leave now Ma."

"Where are you going?"

"Back to the shelter before they close the doors," he said getting up out of his chair while putting on his jacket.

"That light jacket is going to act like a parachute when the wind blows. Sit down you haven't even eaten yet. I want you to stay here tonight."

"What about Justine and Kevin?"

"How many times have I told you they don't run me? This is my house! And I do what I want in my house. Besides, they don't live here. They better pay more attention to their own families and let me handle mine."

"Ok Ma. So what you cook anyway?"

"Food, go wash your hands and set the table."

Tim hesitates before he goes to wash his hands, he watches his mother move around the kitchen with ease but a little slower than usual. She still has a knot on her head and it has affected her motor skills a little. When she hit the ground, not only did she hit her head but injured her shoulder and hips too. She tried not to be obvious when in pain but couldn't help but flinch now and then. She can still cook and that's all that matters to her. Timothy watched her for a few more seconds then goes to the bathroom and washes his hands. He looks up and sees his reflection and grimaces. He's a skeleton! He walks out the bathroom to find his food and his mother's food on the table. She was putting ice in the glasses, for Kool-Aid she made, to bring to the table. Timothy rushed over and took the glasses and the pitcher from his mother.

"Ma, can I ask you a question?"

"Didn't you just ask me one?" she asked rhetorically smiling.

"What makes you stick up for me when people are right about me? What makes you love me when everybody else hates me? What makes you almost die for me? I guess I just want to know why you do what you do for me," he said as he hung his head in shame.

"What makes you think a mother's job is ever done? What makes you think I have the right to give up on you? What makes you think I care about who hates you? And what better reason do I have to die for than my child?" she asked with a smile that would warm the skies.

"Ma, I asked you questions for answers, not for more questions!"

They sat there and laughed about that for a few minutes. While Andrea blessed the food Timothy just stared at her. He was very grateful for a wonderful woman like her. He knew that if he had to depend on anybody, it would always be his mother. He ate anything she put in front of him,

65

unlike his siblings that didn't like this or that. When momma made it, Timothy ate it. They ate and talked for what seemed like hours. Afterwards, he helped her clean up just like he used to do when he was a child.

"Tim where do you get the money from to buy your drugs?" she asked while she watched him wash the dishes.

"Odd jobs, laying brick" He didn't flinch answering the questions.

"Laying bricks?" she asked, surprised at his answer.

"Yea, I do brick mason work or carpentry."

"Ok, but how did you get hooked up in that?"

"Dad taught me!" he answered like she should've known that.

"What kind of money can you make doing that?"

"I make great money. I can make a few hundred for a day's work, depending on what they want, and how long it takes me to do it."

"Uh huh, so how often do you get these types of jobs?" Andrea was taking mental notes.

"Mmm, almost every weekend. It pays for my lifestyle. I gotta do it even if I don't want to."

"Ok, where do you get these jobs from?"

Timothy didn't wonder why his mother was asking him these questions. He just loved the time they were spending with each other. It's been a long time since he's been home and he wanted to stay.

"Mr. Jimmy!"

"Why does that name sound familiar?"

"Cause you know him; that was Dad's old friend."

"He was more than your dad's old friend. He was your dad's best friend and best man at our wedding. It's been a very long time since I've seen him. I believe the last time was when your father died. He would've done anything for your father and vice-versa."

"Yea I can tell. He always tells me I'm just like my dad, but not to end up like him."

"Yea that sounds just like old Jimmy. You need to tell him I'm not going to let you end up like your daddy."

"Ok Ma. What else do you wanna know?"

"How much drugs do you buy? How long does it last you?"

"I know you don't know the lingo, so all I'm going to say is, I buy a lot of drugs and I sit and use till it's gone."

"And how long does that take?"

"Usually three or four days"

"So that's when you disappear for about a week?"

"Yea cause I don't eat, sleep or nothing during that time. So when my drugs are done, that's when I'm sleeping finally."

"How long can you go without drugs?"

"I'm trying to build up my stamina right now. The longest I can go is about five days."

"How long has it been so far?"

"You've been out the hospital two days... and the day you went into the hospital makes three... so yea, three days."

"How do you feel?"

"I haven't been thinking about it but I know it's coming around to that time because of how my body starts to feel."

"How does it feel?"

"It's like I haven't eaten for days, there's this terrible hunger. I feel like if I don't get it, I will die. It's like my body takes control and I no longer have any say in it. Everything in me is twisting and turning in knots and I feel like something is wringing me out to dry."

"So it's painful?" she asks, watching her son carefully, watching his every reaction. She's trying to figure out what makes this tick so she can figure out how to help.

"Very painful, unbearable"

"If you get into like a fight or something, does that make you want the drugs even more?"

"Well kinda, I mean if something is bothering me emotionally or if I get to thinking about my past then yea, I will use."

"So your thoughts can drive your addiction?"

"Well I never thought of it like that but I guess you can say that." Timothy was not nervous or uncomfortable about speaking about his addiction to his mother. He was tired of lying. What exactly was he lying about? She knew he was an addict. She just didn't know what that meant except he loved drugs. Being an addict didn't mean he loved drugs, he hated them. His body loved them. His cells needed them to survive, or so it felt. If freedom meant telling the truth about everything then he was willing to tell it all.

"What would you do for a high?" she asked, not wanting to know what he did, but what lengths he would go to, to get that high.

"Depending on if I'm feenin or not. If I'm real bad then you can say I would basically do anything for a high but if not then I would do only what's necessary."

"Ok like working if you're not fiending or robbing somebody if you are?"

"Yea, something like that," Timothy answered, not wanting her to look at him as a robber since this is what happened to her three days ago.

"Ok. Do you like the way you feel when you're high?"

"It's not whether I like it or not. I hate it but my body needs it. It doesn't matter if I liked the way I feel. To tell you the truth, I don't remember the majority of the time the way I feel to even enjoy the high. I do remember that I feel good, feeding my body."

"So it doesn't really matter that you like what you're feeling? What matters is that your body is satisfied, that you no longer feel the withdrawal symptoms or it's no longer craving."

"Absolutely!"

"Wow, so that totally changed my outlook on being an addict. I mean I used to pray that God would take the desire and the enjoyment for this drug from you but what you've just told me is that you really have no enjoyment or desire for this drug but you use it to appease and satisfy your body's desires."

"Yea, whatever you just said" Tim smiled. He wasn't trying to figure out the logical reasoning behind his addiction. He just knew he wanted to stop.

*1 Corinthians 13:4 Charity suffereth long, and is kind; charity envieth not; charity vaunteth not itself, is not puffed up,*

*1 Corinthians 13:8 Charity (love) never faileth:*

Travis is in his garage putting up shelves; his marriage is shaky right now. He feels as if he's walking on egg shells because of his extra marital affair. Christine insists on fighting through this even though it's hard. She knows it's going to take God to teach her how to trust again. All week she thought of ways that she may have failed as a wife to fulfill the needs of her husband. What could she have done different? They started going to counseling to find out what are the necessary steps they have to take in order to save their marriage. The one thing she was afraid of is if a baby was on the way. He whole heartedly assured her there wasn't. This is when thoughts began to surface, thoughts of her brothers making fun of him, her mother making slick remarks. She made remarks of Christine's husband being sweet, gay, or homosexual; whatever you wanted to call it. She wasn't blind, she seen the feminine ways he had, the way he twisted when he walked. He would catch himself and correct it. She even had gay friends that tried to tell her that he was gay, but she wouldn't listen. Now she questioned it more and more every day. She believed he loved her, but was he undercover? Was he a down low man? The thoughts would make her angry, and then upset. She loved him but could she stay in the marriage knowing he stepped out with another man? Travis knew what his wife was thinking. He tried hard to be the man she wanted and needed him to be. He simply did not want her to know it was with a man he cheated on her with but not just any man, one of the most celebrated spiritual powerhouses of their time.

The counselor worked hard to establish a root for the infidelity, but pulling the truth out of Travis was like pulling the root from a hundred year old oak tree. During these sessions, Christine learned things about her husband and his family that she never knew. She had to look at her husband in a different light, which began to shed light on their marriage. He was a man in desperate need of help and he didn't even know it. He was taught to be taken advantage of by men, so he could never be the man he. He was raped and continually molested, as a child by those whom he trusted so even though he didn't like it, he was basically taught this was life. Travis didn't know who he was, much less, knew why he did what he did.

The pastor marveled at how he could live such a normal life to natural eyes, but to spiritual eyes he was covered with so many fig leaves it would take Adam to pull them all off. He is willing though and that's a start, but is he willing to tell the truth about what really happened? The answer came one session as he was pushed into the fire. He had to trust God or he felt as if he would die. The truth came out in a whisper, she heard it and cried. He assured her he loved only her and that it was the first and last time. He was scared. Was this it? Was she going to go to the lawyer next? God had different plans even in his garage; God shows His love.

"Travis, I can't explain the pain I'm feeling from what I've learned. At the same time I can't imagine the pain you've felt going through what you did growing up. I have every right to divorce you, take my child and start a new life without you. But I'm not; we will work through this. I intend on fighting until I have no breath left in my body. God told me you were my husband. Seeing as how I trust HIM, I know HE did not make a mistake-YOU did!" she pointed at him, tears welling up in her eyes. Travis already had streams forming down his cheeks. She took a breath in between words.

"I will forgive you, but you must earn my trust. You've betrayed me but I believe you're sorry. I believe you won't do it again but that's not the point. The point is you've done it when you shouldn't have. I know God works in ways we can't imagine. And all of this probably happened to get what was filthy in you, out of you. You needed this; you needed to heal even at the cost of my wound. I will heal eventually but you needed your wounds opened so that you can be the man God called you to be. I will stand with you until you get there. But please understand this, I'm no fool. You try this again, I'll cut you and gut you and leave you flopping like a fish. Do you understand what I'm telling you?"

"Yes" he whispered, barely looking at her in her eyes.

"Now this is our business, our family business. Nobody else has to be included in this mess. We will work this out between us, our counselors and God. But it's time for you to separate from all your sissy friends and from all your female friends. You need to hang around more Godly men that's doing something with their lives."

"Ok" again he whispered. She meant the world to him; her and his baby. He would do whatever she said to keep her in his life. Just like her, God told him she was his wife. He didn't want to and now knows he wouldn't be losing her. Christine walked away. Travis breathed a sigh of relief. He knew this was not going to be easy. He knew things would have to be sacrificed but whatever he had to do, he was ready to do it. All he could do was look up to heaven and smile, God did it again!

# CHAPTER 6

*James 5:15* *And the prayer of faith shall save the sick, and the Lord shall raise him up; and if he have committed sins, they shall be forgiven him.*

Karen enjoyed herself so much at church that night that she kept going back. Her prayers are being answered. The tubes were taken out of Shawn and he can talk. The police had been there and questioned him several times but he doesn't know who shot him. All he could tell them was that a blacked out Crown Victoria was where the bullets came from. He never admitted to them of his drug activity. They asked but he always denied it. He said was meeting up with some "friends" and they were suppose to go out that night.

The only part that may have resembled the truth was that he was on the phone with one of his friends when he dropped the phone and ran. Karen wasn't stupid she knew the truth. She might live in the suburbs, but she grew up in the streets. Karen asked Officer Preston to take her to where Shawn was shot. Instantly she knew what he was doing out there. She saw the caliber of people that was out there. She saw the crack vials and drug transactions that went on without fear of authority. She saw the cars, the jewelry, and the guys gambling by the corner store flashing their piece to thwart cheaters. She saw what she didn't want to believe. She knew Shawn wasn't there to meet friends but to sell drugs. How long has he been doing this and why?  She searched her mind for the answers to these questions, but could not find one.

Karen knew this place as the "jungle".  This was a place she avoided growing up, because of the fear of becoming comfortable in a mess.  She had friends from school who would hang out here but would be found dead days later.  This was a place she didn't come to as an adult.  She knew the dangers of the jungle.  What she couldn't figure out is how Shawn found his way out here.

They lived clear on the other side of town.  Who taught him how to hustle? Who taught him about this life that she tried to forget?  Shawn was in a lot of pain.  He lost sight in his right eye.  He has a rod and a few pins and screws holding his leg together.  He had fifty percent use of his right shoulder and his spine was intact but bruised.  He had several swollen discs but at least he was going to be able to walk again which was the best news of it all.  Karen stared at her only child as he ate.  His father sold drugs in his younger years but there's no way he could know that, heck he barely knew his father.

"Momma, you been standing there staring at me for twenty minutes, what's up?"  He said, continuing eating, not bothering to look up.

"I'm just trying to figure out where I went wrong at Shawn."

"What are you talking about Mom? This has nothing to do with you" he said, turning so he could look at her out of his left eye.

"Shawn did a bullet damage your brain? Because when it has something to do with you, then it has something to do with me" she said closing the gap between her and him.

"Ma, all I'm saying is it's not your fault. It's a decision I made."

"Ok since you say that then, what made you make that decision Shawn? Was it because your dad wasn't there, and somebody told you they were going to father you but you have to sell? Or is it because I wasn't there; because of Granny's death? What Shawn? Because inquiring minds wants to know. Oh and please don't lie, I've been there. I know what goes on over there. I know you selling. You can lie to everyone else but don't you dare lie to me. Not with all that I had to go through." She stood directly in front of him. He watched her; he watched her eyes looking for something that would allow him to lie. Instead all he found was eyes that searched him for the truth, truth she deserved.

Shawn sat there for a minute. He knew he couldn't lie but life was coming at him a little too fast for his tastes. He was trying to wrap his mind around the fact that his eye is gone, and he can barely walk because of the damage to his leg. He grimaces to think about lifting his right arm and to top it off his back is reminding him of a three-alarm fire because of the burn that was ripping through it.

"Shawn I'm still waiting son," she said matter of factly.

Shawn looks up at his mother. He remembers her tears and fears vividly. There is a time to come clean, and there's no better time than the current.

"I got tired of seeing you do without so I wouldn't have to. I got tired of seeing you come home and pass out at the kitchen table and I slept in my bed all night. I watched you scrape change for a soda but would spend your paycheck keeping me in comfort. I saw you wear the same dress but I had a new pair of kicks and Sean John jeans every week costing seventy five to a hundred dollars. I saw what honest money did for honest people...NOTHING! So I started slanging. I figured the less I'm depending on you, the more likely you were to quit one of your jobs. And my daddy, yeah well he hasn't even come to see me, so I know for a fact he wasn't helping you."

All Karen could do was listen, listen with tears running down her face. She tried to stop them but the more she tried to the more she cried. Shawn didn't understand she'd rather live without and supply his needs than to not sacrifice and he died anyway. To hear her son put life like that made her understand, not condone, but she understands what he saw. She was able to glimpse life through his eyes by his words. He was right, not only was his father not helping, but he never helped!

"Shawn you're my life and making sacrifices is simply what mothers do. Had you died, I don't think I would've been able to live because it would've all been in vain. This is what I was working so hard to avoid and it happened anyway. I tried to give you the world Shawn but it wasn't mine to give. I tried to give you everything but it still wasn't enough." she said as the tears kept flowing like rivers.

Shawn beckons his mother over to him. He pulls her close to his face to wipe away her tears. She smiles.

"Ma, you're all I have so I already got the world. I got everything Ma! That's why you couldn't give it to me. You actually took it away when you got that second job. I know this will probably make things worse on you now and for that I'm sorry. That was certainly not my intent. The way my mind was thinking may not make sense to you but it did to me. I thought I was helping. I knew I was doing wrong selling but I just figured the money I got from slinging would cause you to stop spending so much money on me. I thought if I had my own money then you could do something that you wanted to do with your paycheck."

"Shawn, I understand that logic. I probably would've thought the same way. But Shawn how were you going to get the money past me? Were you going to lie about a job; because one lie has to be compounded by another? Eventually the truth would have had to come out, then what? Have you ever thought that regardless of the money or how tired I am, that I didn't mind? Have you ever thought that because it's for you, everything I do is worth it? You can't look at things one sided and make decisions based on a one sided view, that's not wisdom son. How hard would it have been to come and talk to me? Instead you made a decision that nearly cost you your life, now what?"

"I know Ma, so where do we go from here?" he asked with his head hung.

Karen grabbed her sons face and turned it towards her own and smiled. "We're going forward son, forward!"

Shawn let his pride go at that point, tears left his eyes quickly. All he could do is apologize profusely, but Karen knew he was sorry. She just wasn't going to allow him to continue to be sorry. What happened has already passed and she was intending to keep it that way. She was holding her miracle child and the world didn't seem so dark anymore. She remembers the sermon that was preached at church the Sunday before. The pastor said, "When the clouds come out, we don't panic because we know the s-u-n is still there. Well, when the clouds of life come out, be not afraid because the S-O-N is still there. You might not see it, but you can feel it's warmth through those clouds. Know that Jesus is never far, you may not see HIM but you can definitely feel his love through those clouds." She felt HIM as she held her child and smiled. She nodded in pleasure, she felt HIM.

"Yea girl, you know how I do. I keep my own thang going. So what you wanna do tonight? I was thinking maybe you could come over here and spend the night tonight, do what grown folks do. You know what I'm saying?" Michael said as he laid comfortably on his couch talking to his new conquest. As she is speaking the phone beeps, the numbers blocked "Hey baby, hold on for a minute," he clicks over.

"Hello?" he answered unsure

" Hi Michael, heard you've been looking for me, wassup?"

"Sondra?" he said sitting up "wassup baby, where you been at? Oh wait, hold that thought I got somebody on the other line. Hold on." He didn't give her a chance to say she would call him back he clicked over so fast.

"Sondra? You there?"

"Yes, Michael."

"So wassup with you? What you been doing with yourself?" he asked, now pacing the floor.

"I'm good, working hard as usual and just been chilling. I got several calls from some of our common acquaintances about you looking for me. Where are you looking for me and most importantly, why are you looking for me?"

"What do you mean? I miss my woman and I want her to come back home. Look whatever happened; we're grown enough to work through it."

"You don't even know what to work through Mike."

"You want to be married and I didn't. I think I was just being selfish trying to hold on to my single life but baby I'm ready now. Just to show you how serious I am, let's go get our license. Let's go to the justice of peace and sign the papers that make us Mr. and Mrs. and start our life together."

"Really," more of a statement than a question.

"Absolutely! Look I'm for real here. Whatever dude you seeing tell him it's over, you going back to your real man."

"It's amazing how you want to act like a real man when I'm gone Michael," voice still calm, but sharp.

"Hold up, hold up." he said holding his hand up "Sondra I was a real man when you was here. I might have been a little nervous about the marriage thing but I'm confident now. If anything, I've grown since you've been gone but I've always been a man."

"It's funny how you think what's between your legs makes you a man. If that were so, I should have been satisfied every minute of the day."

"Oh so you're just going to attack my manhood now?"

"No Michael. I just want you to see that your manhood was never in question, at least not the part that's below your hips. What I questioned is whether or not your manhood was designated for me."

"Ummm you lost me there."

"I know. All I'm saying is that marriage to you is no longer an option for me," she exhaled as she said that. She felt as if a boulder was lifted off of her shoulders.

"What the hell is that supposed to mean? Marriage to me is no longer an option!" he repeated "oh so all of a sudden you don't want to be married? Who you messing with Sondra?"

"This has nothing to do with anyone else Mike. Since I've had time to think and reflect on my life, I've realized that I have been on the wrong path all along. It's time for me to get back going the right way. Back to my original statement, no, marriage is not an option right now."

"Hold up, I'm confused. The whole reason you left is because you wanted to be married and now that you're gone you don't want to be married?" he said rubbing his goatee.

"Mike I told you before I left that I was out on the whole marrying thing anyway. I left because of priorities."

"I'm your priority Sondra!" he yelled.

"You were and that's why I had to leave. There were other important things and people in my life that I put on the back burners for you, and you didn't even appreciate that. I had to leave so I can see what really matters and what really doesn't," now she's pacing. She waited so long to call him trying to avoid arguing with Michael but she knew she had to call. This was the finale.

"Oh so what you're saying is that I don't matter?"

"No, that's not what I'm saying Michael," she said softly. She knew he was going to ask, she had to tell him. It was now or never.

"So what are you saying Sondra? I'm listening," he said as he sat back down. Something in the pit of his stomach told him he wasn't going to like her answer. He was right.

"I'm saying you matter, just not in my life anymore Michael," tears rolled down her face. This was the man she once loved, and still did. She had to let him go though. She knew he was no good for her. She knew if anybody had the ability to take her out, it was him. She was tired and knew if she wanted things to change, she had to do things differently.

All Michael could do was sit in silence. He knew he lost her and it was his fault. What he couldn't understand is where she got the audacity to do to him what he's done to so many. Dump him! Michael goes from silent to enraged to bitter all in one second.

"That's ok. I'm good with that, glad that I didn't have to waste my money on a ring for a foolish little girl. You know how many women wanted to be where you were? I'm a good provider, good man, and good lover. I took you out the slums and made you a woman. Did you forget that? You were nothing without me, and now you've gone back to your original state...you're nothing now."

"Nice try boy! Only you would think you have the ability to make somebody. I was coming out of those projects with or without you. As I remember, you begged me for weeks to move in with you."

"I don't beg no hoe for nothing.  Everything is given to me!" he said bitterly.

Sondra smiled, she was sure she made the right decision now.  "Michael, I'm not going there with you.  You have a good life.  God bless you and you're in my prayers."

"Keep your prayers, you'll NEVER find another man like me.  No one will put up with you like I did.  You'll come back on your knees!"

"Well I see that this conversation is over.  Be blessed in life Michael.  I'm out," with that Sondra hung up.  As vicious as he was trying to be, it didn't work.  She chose not to give his words life.  She would not give him the power he used to have over her.  Sondra laughed.  She was going to enjoy her new life.

Michael is seething with rage.  How dare she dump him?  What nerve did she have to leave him when he decided to marry her, when he finally decided he would do what SHE wanted!  He threw the phone across the room.  He watched it in slow motion make impact with the wall and shatter into hundreds of pieces.  He frowned.  His life was beginning to resemble those pieces.

# CHAPTER 7

*2 Kings 6:17* *And Elisha prayed, and said, Lord, I pray thee, open his eyes, that he may see. And the Lord opened the eyes of the young man...*

*1 Corinthians 10:13* *There hath no temptation taken you but such as is common to man: but God is faithful, who will not suffer you to be tempted above that ye are able; but will with the temptation also make a way to escape, that ye may be able to bear it.*

Tim was on the block again. It has been five days since the incident with his mother and his body is starting to manifest the signs of the addiction. He desperately needed to find Paul. He had to have the drugs one last time before he went through the worst hell imaginable- at least to him it was. This is the block where people come to either lose their lives or die. Timothy knew the difference. He lost his life right here on these streets. Everything he was building, every dream he had; they were all lost. NFL-lost, college-lost, scholarships-lost. People who lost their lives out here generally didn't die, they just wanted to. Tim's steps were brisk at first but as he began to take in his surroundings they slowed. The block used to be a place to get all of his needs taken care of. Instead he felt a sense of darkness there. He looked up to see only blue skies and a bright sun but when he looked back at his surroundings, he sensed clouds and raging storms.

He looked across the street and saw a familiar sight, a drug transaction but this time he couldn't move. For some reason his legs wouldn't go to the left or the right, and his eyes wouldn't move off of the young man that bought the drugs. He was about Tim's age and his build; might be a few inches shorter. Tim watched the kid look around nervously then go into the door of the apartment building. This young man couldn't even wait to get into an apartment to get his fix. The young man lit up right in the doorway of the apartment building. He inhaled the lethal poison into his lungs, and his chest exhaled; he slid down the wall and closed his eyes as if he was no longer present in this natural world. Tim watched attentively as a mother and her child cross over the young man's body in order to exit the apartments. The child just stared, but the mother knowing and fully accepting this as a way and part of life kept going.

Tim felt like crying, why did he see this? His feet started moving again, but he couldn't help but to notice the junkies and the way they moved-they were fidgety, always jerking and nervous. They were paranoid about everything. Some of their teeth were brown and breath was foul because they didn't bother to brush them anymore. Their hair was uncombed, matted and dirty. Their clothes were ripped, nasty and stinking. He watched as the professionals in the Benz and BMW's came through as well. They had a better handle on things, but nonetheless, they were junkies. They just looked better and had high paying jobs. All Tim could think of was that he was no better; he was just like them. Why was he judging then? He couldn't understand but something in his heart kept telling him he wasn't. He turned around trying to find that quiet voice, but couldn't.

85

He just thought it was his body going through withdrawal that he was hearing voices. He started to walk again, he didn't notice he stopped once more because life kept moving around him or was it just dying around him?

He passed some dealers and noticed how they served their customers but turned around and laughed at them. They would even laugh in their faces or throw their drugs down causing the addict to get on all fours to find what they so badly needed. Some would even abuse the addicts and ridicule them. All the things Paul did to him, and yet here he was looking for more. More of the shame, the embarrassing and derogatory names that he was called; the gun threats, of being spit on and being treated like trash. He stopped walking. He didn't want more. Out of his peripheral, he saw a bright object move close to him. The sun was reflecting off the object so much it caused him to blink rapidly and caused his head to jerk backward. When he turned to see what it was, he felt the cold steel barrel pressed against his cheek in broad daylight.

"You walking round here like you a snitch boy. You working for the cops?"

"I'm not working for anybody and no I'm not a snitch." The guy was looking him up and down with a deep scowl on his face like he was angry about something. Tim wasn't afraid though, he didn't know why but even with the gun in his face, he knew he wasn't going to die.

"I remember you, you Paul's do boy! You look different without that glass pacifier in your mouth. What you doing watching people like you boss or something?"

"I'm looking for Paul."

"I know what you looking for, I got it right here," he said patting his pocket with his left hand as he still held the gun to Tim's face with the right.

Tim shook his head. He was disgusted but wasn't sure what to do. He looked into the face of this angry person and decided right then he didn't want any more. "I don't need anything."

"Oh, so you faithful huh? Well good for you, but tell ya boy, black said, 'I'm going to ventilate you and his cranium the next time I see ya'll,' ya hear me?"

A frown creased Tim's forehead. It's now or never time. "Dude since you so boss, do it yourself. What, you scared of Paul that you gotta deliver a message through me? Black? Go tell Paul what Black said, then let's see exactly how boss you are!" Black was so angry at that response that he tried to shoot Tim, but his gun jammed. He paid so much attention to his gun that he didn't notice the kid walking away. He watched him intently, couldn't figure out why he didn't go after him or even pistol-whip him when he had the chance.

Tim hit the corner and before he turned it, he looked back one last time. He decided no matter the hell, pain, and anguish, no matter what he had to do or go through, he wasn't coming back here. He wanted to live again. He knew what he had to do. It was day five, day six was going to be much worse but he had to endure it. When Tim made it back to the house, Andrea grabbed him and looked at his arms for fresh needle tracks, his nose for traces of powder, went through his pockets for the drugs and found forty dollars. She was confused.

"Where'd you get the money?" she asked, looking into his eyes.

"Laid some bricks in a lady's yard," he answered nonchalantly.

"Where you been at?" she asked, as she sat down at the kitchen table.

"On the block, trying to satisfy this hunger."

"Timothy, I don't know much about your world, but I do know that you don't leave with money and come back with money, not when you're an addict."

"I don't want to do it no more. I'm not going to do it no more. I know what lies ahead of me and I don't want to do it but I got to."

"What do I need to do? I want to help. Maybe we can go to one of those places? They at least can ease the effects of the withdrawal."

"While forming an addiction to another drug? Nope, that won't work."

"Dr. Livingston can help; he deals with stuff like this all the time. He will come over here and help," she said worried as any mother would be.

"Fine. Have Doc come over but don't give me anything. I just gotta go through this."

"What you mean, don't give you anything? Am I supposed to watch you go through excruciating pain and not do anything about it?"

Timothy smiled through the pain. It has already started. His body is beginning to protest his decision to not feed it, what it so badly needs. He touches his mother face, trying to ease her mind about the situation. "I don't have to do this here. I can go elsewhere and come back when I'm done."

"No! You're my son and I'm going to see you through this every step of the way."

"Alright then, my only request is that you pray Ma. Pray hard every day cause I don't want to die!"

"And you're not!!!" she exclaimed as she rose up from her chair. Tim watched her walk down the hallway to her room, grabbed her coat and hat and came flying back down the hallway. Tim smiled to himself, that's the fastest he's ever seen her move. She grabbed him and they left hurriedly out the door and walked the eight blocks to the church without speaking to anyone.

"Here's what's going to happen," she turned him around to face her outside of the church. "I'm going to talk to some of these guys that have been through what you are about to go through, and get advice and possibly some help from them. Now I'm willing to put everything on the line for you. I brought you back into my house against everybody's wishes. The least you could do is when you come out, you come to counseling every week until I'M convinced you're not going back. I've been a fool many times before Timothy. I'm tired of it and I'm not going to be made a fool now. You sure you want to go through with this?" she asked intently.

Timothy knew Andrea didn't see what he saw today. He never told her about "Black" either or she would've flipped out. She didn't know what it did to him to finally open his eyes and see things as they really were. He wasn't going back. He decided he wasn't going to die an addict. He was determined to not only keep his sanity but he wasn't about to make his mother or himself look like a fool. He's had enough of that.

"Ma, my decision is made. I'm going through this and when I come out I will go to counseling until you're convinced I'm staying clean. Do you know how many drug dealers are on the block? I could've gotten drugs from anyone of them but I didn't. Instead, I came back home with the forty dollars and now here I am. I think you can say I'm pretty serious."

Andrea had to nod in agreement. What he said was truth. He could've bought the drugs from anybody but he didn't. No fresh needle marks or powder up his nose. She wanted to trust him but most importantly, she HAD to trust God. They went inside the church and spoke to the pastor before church service began. After service, he called them into his office along with some other guys who've been through what Timothy was about to do.

They advised her on what to expect and they even promised they would be there with her every day until he came out. The pastor told her he would come and help as much as he could and he would cancel all just to help. He explained to Timothy that many years before, he was in the same boat and he had a passion for people struggling with addictions. Timothy finally had someone who knew and understood what it felt like to be an addict but make it out and become successful. He had a target point, now he felt like he could do this and come out. He caught a glimpse of himself as he was leaving. He hated what he seen but he stood there and stared any way. The reason: change is on the way.

*Mark 14:38 Watch ye and pray, lest ye enter into temptation. The spirit truly is ready, but the flesh is weak*

.

"So you quit your second job-now what? It's going to take more than you quitting your job to keep Shawn off those streets. Because frankly speaking Karen, the devil don't care about the sacrifices you make if they're not unto God!" Sam said.

"Ok Sam, then what can I do to keep him off the streets? I mean I don't even understand because Shawn wasn't raised in or near the streets, so how did he learn to hustle?" Karen asked curiously.

"Karen just because you don't go to the streets don't mean they don't come to you. How many street vendors or bootleg artists have you seen in your neck of the woods?" he asked.

"Plenty." she answered.

"You think they live there?"

"No, I guess they just come where they feel the money is at."

"Ok, good, but the truth is they do live there. Just because you're out of the projects physically, doesn't mean you're out of them mentally. You can have someone living in a half a million-dollar house, yet the house look like garbage. When you walk into their house, it's filthy. It's not that they don't have the ability to clean, it's just they don't have the mentality to own a half a million dollar house but yet they have one," he explained.

"Ok Sam, I kinda understand but then again, there's something there that I'm just not getting."

"Ok put it this way, your neighbor could have come from the worst projects and have the APPEARANCE of a successful business man, but the truth is he may have made his money scamming people out of their money. All I'm saying is looks are deceiving. Shawn could've gotten hooked up with the nice young man from down the street that said, 'yes ma'am, no ma'am, thank you ma'am, no thank you ma'am.' Wore dockers and button down shirts, carried his bible, never late to Sunday school, but is the biggest drug dealer this here side of creation!" he explained.

"Sam you've just described ninety eight percent of his friends." Karen was beginning to understand what Sam was saying.

"Karen, somebody introduced Shawn to this lifestyle. They saw a weakness and they exploited it, so now Shawn knows he has a weakness or a void in a specific area. They come up with a plan to fix or fill that void. Oh so your mom works all these hours and you don't get to see her- that's the exploitation of the weakness. So now he's like yeah, I don't get to see her at all- now he's aware of the void. Ok well if she quits then you won't get all the nice stuff you're used to so here's how you fix that; sell drugs and make the money yourself, tax free (because of course they have to state the benefits) and your mom can quit. You can spend more time with her and still have all the money and more with her doing less. There's the plan to fix or fill the void."

"Dang Sam! You make it sound so easy," she said in shock.

"Karen this isn't new to me. It happened to me myself and to you. We just have to know what to do when we see it happening to our children."

"But that's the problem Sam, I didn't see it. So what do I do now?" Karen was listening intently.

"To tell you the truth Karen, I don't know. But I know who does and I will seek HIM in prayer. Meanwhile Karen, you have to start guiding Shawn down a different road."

"And how do I do that?" she asked.

"YOU have to be led by God, once he sees your steps being guided then he will follow you," he answered.

"Ok now so how do I train him?" she inquired.

"Training up a child in the way he must go, like it says in Proverbs 22:6, means that he has to see you following God, you have to train a child by doing."

"Sam, Shawn isn't exactly a child anymore, he's almost a man."

"First of all, just because he's almost eighteen doesn't make him a man. He has a lot to learn about being a man, and if he doesn't have anyone there that can teach him, then he'll be like most men that never learn. Secondly, he can still be trained but it doesn't start with him, it starts with you."

"Ok so in your opinion you don't feel like a woman can teach a boy to be a man," she asked but stated it at the same time.

"I feel like a woman can show a young man some things, but there are things about a man that a woman cannot relate to. I can't teach my daughter how to be a woman but I can show her how a man is supposed to treat a woman. I had no idea about periods and training bras and cramps but my wife knew because it was a part of her. It's the same with men."

"Sam I think you're the first man that explained that in a way that I can understand. You know what you are talking about. Ok, so I'm coming to church and I figure my next step is salvation but then what?"

"Ok what does salvation mean to you?" he asked.

"It means I'm not going to hell. I'm being saved from going into that fire that I've heard so much about," she answered truthfully.

"Salvation is actually not about heaven or hell. Salvation is an introduction into a relationship. It's a formal introduction to a King that holds both heaven and hell in his hands. As you become closer to HIM you realize that you're not from earth, but you're from where HE is. The more you get closer to God is the more you realize that you have a home in heaven, but you're away on assignment," he explained.

"Wow," she said in amazement "When you explain it like that, it's like you're describing a dignitary or something."

"What I actually described would be considered a foreign dignitary called an ambassador."

"So when I get saved, I become an ambassador?" she asked.

"No, you go into training to become one."

"And what does this training consist of?"

"An ambassador first must learn the laws of his land. The ambassador of China couldn't be in another country if he didn't know the laws of his own country." He answered

"Why wouldn't he need to know the laws of the other country? I mean he is going to be living there!" she asked.

"The ambassador knows he has something called diplomatic immunity but he also knows he represents a whole country or kingdom. So he or she will not do anything to bring shame on those he represents."

"What if he broke a law that he didn't even know he was breaking? I mean I understand that what you're telling me is about salvation and stuff but really if I'm going to be saved, I want to know how to do it right and what the repercussions are for mistakes."

"Something done unintentionally can be excused by the King as long as when you find out about it you go straight to the King."

"So if I messed up unintentionally I can go to God and He'll do what?"

"Karen, you're asking a lot of questions about something you haven't even stepped into yet," he said.

"I just want to know what I'm getting into that's all," she replied.

"The only thing that you're going to get into is a relationship," he said.

"Ok one more question?" she asked

"Alright one more, what is it?"

"What is repentance? I mean is it just about saying you're sorry? Like if I had sex; do I just keep saying sorry till I stop having sex or what?"

"Repentance is not just about you saying you're sorry. There has to be a change of mind that happens. When you say you're sorry for having sex, you have to change your mind about it as well so when the temptation does pop up again, it won't affect you."

"Ok so how do I change my mind about it?"

"I thought you said one more?" he smiled.

"Ok but this the last one, I promise," she laughed.

"You have to understand why it's wrong to have sex outside of marriage. You have to understand why God says not to do it. Once you know why and understand the reasoning of God, then you can say ok my mind is changed and I won't do it again."

"Hmmm, you make everything sound so, ummm, not difficult. I won't say easy because I know it's not but it doesn't sound like something I wouldn't be able to do."

"It is absolutely something you will be able to do and just imagine, once you start going down the right path, your son will follow. I'm not saying that it's going to be easy and without hurdles but God will give you the strength to jump over them."

"Sam can I ask you a personal question," she asked shyly.

"Oooohhhh Lawwwwd have mercy. Lord she promised the last question would be the last and it's not. Jesus save me pleeeeeeease," he said playfully.

Karen laughed; she thoroughly enjoyed talking to Sam. He made her laugh at the same time educating her. She felt comfortable in front of him and speaking to him on the phone. Karen imagined she could be with him but he mentioned a wife, she wanted to know more. Why didn't he talk about her more and how can he talk to her so much and she not say anything?

"Ok you laughed but then you got quiet. Must be a serious question. Well go ahead, let's hear it," he was curious now.

"Ok since you got jokes about me questioning you, I won't ask you a question but instead I want you to tell me about your wife."

The statement surprised Sam. Was he ready to speak of her? Was he ready to experience the emotions and pain that he suppressed for so long?

"My wife was a great woman. She was a woman who stood on her faith no matter how things looked. I learned so much from her. She improved me so much that I don't think I would be the man I am today without her."

"You speak of her in past tense, where is she?" she asked curiously. Was he divorced? She thought to herself.

"My wife died six years ago of cancer," he said in a quiet voice.

"OMG!! I'm so sorry Sam, we don't have to talk about it anymore," she said. She wasn't expecting that.

Sam laughed, "it's ok Karen, I don't mind. She's who taught me everything I'm trying to teach you"

"Wow, she must have been an awesome teacher because of the way you explain things," she complimented.

"Thank you," he smiled remembering her. "She was an excellent teacher. She made sure our kids knew what to do before she passed. My kids ended up taking care of me instead of the other way around," he laughed thinking about them.

"How many kids do you have?"

"Four, three boys and a beautiful girl that's the mirror image of her mother," he answered.

"Did she have breast cancer?" she asked "I mean Sam please let me know if I'm being intrusive."

"You're ok and no she had a rare form of lung cancer. The ironic thing is she never smoked a day in her life. I happened to go with her on one of her appointments and was sitting there when the doctor said she had stage four of some cancer that we couldn't pronounce and was told that we need to get her affairs in order and gave us the contact to hospice and said she only had three months left to live."

"Oh my God," she whispered into the phone teary eyes and all.

"She told that doctor that he didn't know what he was talking about and that she was going to show him exactly whose report she was going to listen to," he laughed while telling the story. "She showed him because instead of three months, she lived three years. She knew though and she kept up her sense of humor while preparing us to let her go."

"So she was ready to leave?" she asked.

"Yeah, she was ready. She had an amazing relationship with God that she knew when her time was close and she smiled ear to ear because she knew she was going home. I hated it but I had to let her go. If I had my way I would've raised her from the dead a thousand times. She looked me in my eyes the day before she died, smiled and pointed her little boney finger at me and said you better not. We laughed and laughed that whole day. Everything was so funny, everything I did or said we just laughed at. We got into bed laughing and she told me to just wrap my arms around her and I wrapped her in my arms and we went to sleep. When I woke up she was gone," by this time he had tears in his eyes.

"Oh please don't tell me anymore," she said in between sobs. "That is the most beautiful saddest story I have ever heard."

Sam smiled. "You need Jesus girl," he laughed.

"I know but OMG! Wow, wow, wow is all I can say. I mean the way you talk about her makes me feel the love that you had for her. I already know she was a great woman. I hope to learn more about her just not tonight. That is just too beautiful of a story to tell me in one night. Let's get back to Shawn or something."

Sam was laughing so hard, his stomach and ribs hurt. He had to take several breaths in order to speak again. "Ok well tell me, what does Shawn like to do? How can we get the boy into Church?"

"Ok that's a lot better. Shawn is very creative and loves music. He can play almost any instrument. Of course he can rap and write but I know he loves the technical side of it like making the beats or producing."

"I know a guy in the church that does stuff like that. Let me talk to him, maybe he can take Shawn under his wings."

"Thank you. Sam if you need anything in return just let me know."

"I will never ask you for anything in return. I do this because I simply love God," he stated.

"And I know HE simply loves you too. Hey I'm not asking you out or nothing but I'm cooking tomorrow to take Shawn a plate. I'm tired of him complaining about the hospital food. If you want I can fix you a plate too," she said shyly.

"I would love that, I don't get a chance to cook much. All my kids are grown except my baby boy and he's nineteen and in college and definitely don't have time to eat anything home cooked. I'm mostly at work so that sounds great," Sam said as he licked his lips thinking about home cooked food.

"Ok well I'll call you when I'm finished cooking and see what time and place we can meet up." She was smiling ear to ear thinking of seeing him again. He was a good-looking man after all. Before Sam could respond, his radio went off. Shots fired six blocks away from his current position.

"Well duty calls so I will talk to you tomorrow," he stated.

"Talk to you tomorrow Sam, be safe tonight," she said confirming her expectation of his call.

"Will do, bye!" he said as he hurried off the phone and jumped in his police cruiser, flipped the switch to turn on the sirens and lights. He stopped for a moment to pray then he put his boot to the floor till the cruiser sped off in route to who knows what.

*Matthew 5:38-39* *Ye have heard that it hath been said, An eye for an eye, and a tooth for a tooth: (39) But I say unto you, That ye resist not evil: but whosoever shall smite thee on thy right cheek, turn to him the other also.*

Paul drums his fingers on the kitchen table as he goes through the images in his mind. His imagination has captured and taken him to a place where vengeance is king. He envisions blood-splattered shirts and brains on sidewalks. The images represent what he wants done to those that tried to do the same to him in the few weeks prior. His thoughts are interrupted by a figure that seems to darken his mood every time he sees her. He has one child, a boy that is six months old. This is what happens when you mix business with pleasure.

Paul looks at his child's mother and a look of utter contempt and disgust marks his face. To say he hates her would be a gross understatement. She is one of his many experiments in control. He created a drug addict because she would tell him too many times that she didn't need him. He wanted to prove to her that the very thought of her self-reliance was a lie. She stands there with her hands on her hips, rolling her neck and spitting filth so wicked out of her mouth that the person she speaks to just looks at Paul, shakes his head then walks away.

"Oh so your son and me don't mean anything to you huh playboy?" she asks, focusing her venom on Paul.

"Only you mean nothing to me girl," he spits back.

"Look I don't care how you feel about me, but your son has needs to Paul," she spoke softly this time.

"What happened to all the stuff I sent you? I sent pampers, clothes and formula. Did you smoke that up too?" he said looking at her.

"Paul that was four months ago, PJ is six months old, that stuff is gone! Oh so it's ok to sleep with me, have your baby, get me addicted to your drugs but it's not ok to take care of me?" she was beginning to get mad again.

Paul rose from the table and walked up to her till he was standing at her side and in her ear he whispered, "Remember you didn't need me, what changed your mind whore?" his words were like arrows aimed at a target; it hit.

"Paul you are so nasty, I hate you! Look the only thing I'm asking for is for you to take care of your child. I don't want anything from you for myself. I refuse to keep asking you for drugs because the only reason you give it to me is because you like the control you have over addicts. I'm tired of it," she says calmly.

Paul just eyes her up and down. He has no respect for her at all. He wouldn't even speak her name and threatened that if anybody else spoke her name in front of him, there would be consequences to pay. He yells to one of his boys to bring him some money. He just got in for the sale of some kilos he completed earlier in the day. As the guy hands him the money, she stares at him. Her face wrinkled in confusion, but that won't be for long.

"Here," he said throwing her a stack of money, "that's ten thousand dollars. Take it and leave me alone. Don't call me, don't write me, girl. I don't even wanna see your face ever again in my life," he said as he starts to walk away.

"Oh so this is how you feel about your son? He's only worth ten thousand dollars to you? You know what Paul, do you baby, do you! Because the same people that you treat like garbage, will be the very ones that'll cause your down fall playa," she shot back as she walked out. She is disgusted but she expected nothing less from him. She was actually surprised she got so much from him this time, as he usually would give her a few dollars at a time.

# CHAPTER 8

Sam's sirens and lights are blaring, clearing a way through traffic for him. It seems like it takes him forever to go the six blocks even though the blocks are flying by in a blur. Sam's heart is beating rapidly wondering what kind of scene will he find when he gets there. Finally he pulls up to find two other police cars already there. Sam puts his cruiser in park and sat there for a minute staring at the two bodies that lay in a pool of blood. One is a female; she didn't look much older than his own daughter and the other a young man. The young man was lying face down in a pool of blood, his eyes partially opened. He knew there was no help for him, but apparently the young lady still had a pulse. The EMT's arrived right behind him began working furiously to save her.

Sam stepped out of his car just in time to hear the screams of the relatives and friends of the victims. His brow creased in frustration, "when is this going to stop?" he whispered to himself. As he began to sink deeper into his own thoughts, the voice of one of his peers shook him into reality.

"Hey Sam, we got a witness over here!" the young officer yelled. Sam quickly ran to where a young man about twenty stood shaking. Sam could see the fear coursing through the young man's veins as he stood there staring at the body of his friends or relatives. Sam put his hands on the young man's shoulder and squeezed hard enough to distract the young man and bring his eyes to him. Just then a homicide detective walked up and introduced himself to the young man. Sam was about to leave but the detective thought otherwise.

"Officer Preston, I think you should stay with me on this one."

"Ok Detective Rich," he nodded his head and came and stood by the young man. Sam liked Detective Rich. He was a sixteen year veteran of the police force before joining homicide three years ago. He was thorough and precise. He didn't miss a beat and if he ever did, you can bet he'll come back and catch it. The young man looked as if he would burst with the information he had, so Rich knowing this allowed him to speak.

"What's your name son?" asked Rich.

"Daniel, Sir," the kid answered quietly.

"Daniel, we want to catch the person or people who've done this and I believe you have the information to assist us in doing so. Tell me what happened son. What happened here today? What did you see?"

"Man, that dude shot my cousin man. He shot him for no reason man. That's what happened. I mean I swear man, if I catch that dude man, it's over," he said with a slashing motion to his throat.

"Listen Daniel, do this thing right, let us be the justice. I mean if you go kill this dude, what are you proving? That you're no better than him? That you're a murderer too?" Rich was trying to get the young man to see logically in a sensitive situation.

"Man I know what you saying man, but look at my cousin man. My cousin is dead man, cause he stood up for his wife man. Dude killed him in cold blood man," the young man was starting to become angered. Rich knew how to get control of the situation before it got out of hand though.

"Ok Daniel, who is this dude? What is his name?" Rich asked.

"I don't know his real name. I only know his street name as Black," he said finally giving up a name. Sam immediately got on his radio and asked for any information they can find on the young man named Black.

"Ok son, tell me how this whole thing happened. What made this thing transpire the way it did?"

"Man dude is crazy. He pulled a gun on me across the street cause he wanted some drugs and I didn't have any. Dude went through my pockets and everything. Then when he seen my cousin and his wife, he ran across the street and I ran behind him. He started waving the gun all around trying to holla at my cousin's wife. My cousin was trying to tell dude be easy and everything gonna be alright just put the gun away. Dude started cussing and pushing my cousin trying to get to his wife. My cousin said hey dude, that's my wife, you can't have her. Dude put the gun in my cousin face and said well neither can you and blew my cousin head off. Dude just pulled the trigger for no reason. My cousin ain't even touch dude man." Tears were flowing freely out of Daniel's eyes now.

"How did the wife get shot?" Rich asked.

"She started screaming man, and dude just shot her twice," he said as he ran his fingers across his low cut wavy hair. He looked across the street and seen his family standing there going insane with grief. Rich touched the young man's arm and told him how sorry he was to not only have lost his family but was there to see it happen.

"Man what am I going to do now man? I couldn't even do anything to save him man, him or her. Now I gotta go face my family and tell them what happened," he said as he shook his head.

"Young man, look at me. Daniel, put your eyes on mine for a minute," he said getting the boys attention. "I know today is the hardest and most complex day in your life thus far. And I know the days that are ahead of you are not going to be any easier. I'm going to tell you son, you will need counseling, because what you seen you won't forget. But you can move on from it with the right counseling. I'm going to be right there with you to speak to your family. Daniel, we're gonna catch this guy. You best believe that and you gotta trust me when I tell you that. You have my word that justice will be served this day."

Sam smiled; this is why he liked being around Rich. He knew something was going to get done. They spoke some more and got a full description of what Black was wearing. Instead of taking the boy across the street to his family, Rich instructed Sam to take Daniel downtown to the police station to get a written statement and a recorded statement of what happened. Rich went across the street to speak to the family. As Sam drove off he could hear the family screaming through his windows.

Sam waited patiently to find out what his next orders were. He was sure he was going to be in on the action. He didn't have to wait long. After the detective finished interviewing Daniel for a second time, he came back with a mug shot of this so called 'Black' and his entire arrest record. Sam is amazed at how many times this young man has been to jail in his short life. Black was only twenty-three with four previous felonies for drugs, guns and one for domestic assault. He even had two attempted murder charges against him dropped because the witness's either changed their story or backed out at the last minute.

Detective Rich and his partner briefed the officers and told them where they would find the suspect. There was a new club on the west side of town called Club Fire; fitting place to find a double homicide suspect. Sam got the flyer they were handing out of the suspect, which had a picture of him on it. The whole squad knew Sam was a Godly man so they asked him to pray for their protection, they would need it. Apparently Black was high on some mixture of drugs to the point that he doesn't care about anything, not even life or death.

Sam prayed and when he was done everyone went to prepare for what they had to do. Sam went to his trunk and took out his shotgun and made sure he was locked and loaded. He made sure his sidepiece was loaded as well, just in case he needed to use it tonight. He secured his bulletproof vest in place. He was ready but his heart is pumping and his adrenaline is flowing. Fear tries to creep up but he remembers 2 Timothy 1:7 when it says, *"For God hath not given us the spirit of fear..."* and begins to relax.

Sam is in his cruiser heading to Club Fire. He's never been there but he's heard of it so many times before. As he sits there the reality of everything struck him like a brick thrown at his head, the girl actually died. He shook his head in disgust that both young people lost their lives because of this maniac walking around high on some kind of cocktail of drugs.

His orders were simple, drive pass the club a few times then park in the front but don't get out until he sees the suspect. He pulls up to the club and the beat of the music is causing the windows and windshield to vibrate. The line is literally wrapped around the corner with young men and women dressed in the latest fashion eye balling him. He drives by three times then finally parks across the street with his shotgun sitting in his lap ready for whatever happens.

Club Fire is the hottest club in town. It has three bars, two dance floors-one upstairs and one downstairs. It has above the bar cages with dancers in bikinis, a pole that goes from the ceiling to the floor and the sale of every drug known to man. The club sold the drugs through its independent "dancers" (which are actually dealers girlfriends). Your drug options included: ecstasy, your choice of weed, coke, crack, meth, and even mushrooms. If you can imagine it then they sold it. It was the place to be from Thursday through Sunday if you liked being in that type of environment. And crowded it was, as usual with everybody moving, dancing and gyrating to the music's fast tempo that was bumped through the speakers.

Nobody noticed the menacing appearance of the young man walking with the gun in his waist. He had such a demonic scowl on his face that no one bothered to address him as he pushed his way through the crowd. He didn't care who he pushed whether male or female. He had his eyes fixated on his target and whoever decided to challenge him at this point would never challenge another soul; ever.

Paul sat there in the V.I.P spot with all his boys surrounding him. His girl at the time sitting at his right side and alcohol was all over the table in front of him. He watched the man push his way through the crowd, as his fingers touched the chrome trigger of the weapon that sat in the chair behind his girlfriend. He knew this fellow meant trouble just by the looks of him. He looked at his boy and gave him the signal to intercept the boy before he got close enough to do any harm. Meanwhile, he leaned over and whispered to his girl to leave the club and had one of his boys to escort her out.

Black paid no attention to the woman as she got up to leave but only to the eyes of the man he was after. Just as he approached the booth that sat higher than the rest of the tables, so the world would know you're V.I.P, Paul's boy stepped in front of him with his hands on Black's chest. Black didn't bother to listen to what the man was saying. He just pulled his gun and fired three times into the bodyguard's chest till his dead body slumped down. Then he raised the gun and started firing at Paul while everyone in the club started screaming and running towards the exits. People were jumping over tables, diving under them, using them as shields as they ran out the club. Pandemonium was unleashed. The atmosphere was full of panic and frantic people dashing to and fro.

Sam noticed the people running out the club hysterically. His radio goes off, shots fired inside the club. Sam gets out of his cruiser and stops a young woman running to ask her how many people were shooting. The young lady said she only seen one guy but there may be more. Inside Paul fires back at Black as he's running out the back door. Black is hit and is bleeding profusely, but he feels no pain. He only staggers from the amount of blood loss. Black's finger is still squeezing the trigger but there are no more bullets for the hot weapon to spit out. He looks down and takes the gun out the waist of the first guy he killed. He looks at him and smiles to himself as he begins to recite the words to Tupac's song, Shed So Many Tears. He knew instinctively that this would be his last night on earth and the drugs that were in his system kept the fear from bringing him back to reality. He staggered outside with both guns in either hand.

Samuel looked at the picture on the flyer to make sure he would have the right guy in his sights. When he looked up he saw him, there was no mistaking this guy. Blood was pouring from his body. His white t-shirt was soaking wet and red. Samuel waited till most of the people were out of harm's way before he started his approach. He was hoping this would be a peaceful event. Sam raised his FN tactical shotgun and yelled at Black to "halt and drop his weapons." Black looked at Sam and a menacing smile creased his face. Sam knew then, there was no saving this young man's life tonight.

He was too close to back up and yet not close enough to make the impact his weapon was known for making. Again Sam yelled for him to drop his weapons, but this time Black started to walk towards him, so he froze. His heart started to race but a few deep breaths calmed it down. Just as Black got close enough to the officer in his path, he raised both guns. That was the last thing he would do. Sam fired his shotgun and it hit Black in his chest. Black was able to fire back just before his guns fell from his hands. At the same time, Sam got another shot off as well. Both went down this time.

Sam got hit, he was trying not to go into shock but he can feel the blood flowing like a river down his neck. Another officer came over and dragged him to the safety of the ambulance while the other officers approached Black to check for signs of life. There was none.

# CHAPTER 9

*Psalms 23:3* *He restores my soul and leads me into the path of righteousness for His name sake*

*1 John 4:1* *Beloved, believe not every spirit, but try the spirits whether they are of God: because many false prophets are gone out into the world.*

This was Travis and Christine's last Sunday at the Bishop's church. One of the Elders opened their own church and asked the couple to join them in which they quickly agreed. Travis was deep in thought when his eyes caught sight of Tyrone sitting up behind the pulpit in the "holy chairs" as Travis likes to call them. He's laughing and joking with the Bishop and the other ministers who are too enthralled by his charismatic ways to notice that something just wasn't right about him. Bishop speaks so highly of him, in his eyes, Tyrone could do no wrong. His wife has completely stopped speaking to them but that's ok with Christine, she had a feeling nothing was real about them anyway.

Tyrone was at the top of his game. He was preaching for ALL the mega ministries, headlining at all the big name conferences or had front row V.I.P seats next to the biggest names in the gospel industry. Travis always wondered, 'when did gospel or church for that matter become an industry?' No matter where Tyrone went, he had the best of everything. He had men, women, food, clothes and jewelry and let's not forget the money. The man had beaucoup money. His name was out there; he was dynamic and proved he could get results. So whatever price he would deem necessary for his appearance is the price he would get plus some.

To Tyrone, Travis will always be weak, and be beneath him. He will always be wearing clothes made in China, while Tyrone's was hand made by Italian designers. To him, Travis is a nobody and his child will grow to be like his father, nobody. Tyrone believed Travis' weakness came from how easily he was to be overcome by conscience, so easily convicted. Tyrone thought very low of Travis that as he watched him play with his son, he shook his head in disgust thinking, "he was made to serve and be a slave and I'm made to rule over fools like him." The God he serves knows that a man has his weaknesses. That's why he didn't kill Adam in the Garden of Eden. He did everything God asked, he was allowed to have his passions. Nobody had to know about them, he was good like that.

Travis smiles as he watches Tyrone scoff at him and look away. Travis and Christine are excited about moving churches. For Christine, the new church is closer to home and smaller plus it's much friendlier and more personal. For Travis, it's a chance to start over, to leave the past behind and move forward finally. It was a chance for him to focus on becoming the man God called him to be, so he can be the husband and father his wife and son needs him to be. God had already started the work in him. HE was renovating Travis' temple to be fit to carry HIS Glory. Before they could leave Bishop wanted to speak to them again.

"Travis and Christine, God bless you both for going with the Elder to help them start this new chapter in their life. I pray a new chapter begins in yours as well." Bishop says as he shakes Travis' hand.

"Thank you Bishop, we appreciate everything you've done for me and my family. And yes this is a new chapter in our life." Travis answers.

"Boy, don't you ever forget where home is. If you have any problems you call me."

Travis smiles, "Yes sir, but I don't anticipate any problems."

"I know what you're saying but problems do happen. I've had a lot in this church. I tell you what Travis, it was especially bad in those early years. You get all kind of riff raff in the church. You don't know who's for you or against you and you darn sure don't know who to trust. So to start out with the two of you is a good thing I must say," Bishop explained.

In that moment Bishop was talking, Travis could understand why he couldn't see anything wrong with Tyrone. If you say you were for him and he could trust you then he couldn't see because those things caused blindness in him.

"Well thank you Bishop, my wife and I appreciate you and your family. We're going to miss you guys but I'm sure we'll see each other from time to time," Travis said politely. He shook the Bishops hand again while Christine hugged him in preparation for their departure.

"Well, wait a minute," Bishop yelled behind them as they began to walk away. Tyrone turned to see what Bishop was going to do. He was curious since him and Bishop was supposed to go to dinner after church.

"Heck lookie here, since the wife and kids are out of town, and it's just me and Evangelist Baxter going to dinner, why don't you and your beautiful wife accompany us tonight?" he asked.

Before Travis could stutter to get an excuse out as to why they must turn down the Bishops invitation, Christine stepped forward.

"Oh Bishop, I'm sorry we have to decline. I wish we would've known a little earlier. My mom is going to keep TJ so that Travis and I can have a romantic night out. My mom already made reservations for us and won't tell us where till we drop the baby off," she said smiling, with a look of regret on her face.

"Well there's no reason to be sorry for that Miss Lady. I wish more people would spend time with their spouse like that. You two go and enjoy your time together without the little one. Maybe some other time in the near future we'll get this opportunity again. I told Elder to have you busy. You've been an armor bearer for a long time. You need to know what to do in the role of a minister now. Well get to going. You two have a good time but be careful, romantic nights alone is what caused me to have six kids," he said as they laughed together. Everything Christine said was the truth but she would've lied, if she had to, just so they wouldn't be around that man Tyrone.

Tyrone breathed a sigh of relief; he didn't want to have to cancel dinner because of Travis and his family. He wondered if Christine knew about him because of the way she was eyeballing him. Not one move did he make that she didn't catch. He could feel her eyes on him to the point when he looked at her, she didn't bother to turn away. Tyrone smiled to himself, what if she didn't know but was just interested in him. He didn't blame her. She was

115

married to a sniveling weakling of a man. She deserved a real man, a man who knew who he was and where he was going. She deserved a man that could satisfy her for hours and disappear for days and she would still be ok. He would make sure she knew; he was that man.

*Isaiah 41:10 Fear thou not; for I am with thee: be not dismayed; for I am thy God: I will strengthen thee; yea, I will help thee; yea, I will uphold thee with the right hand of my righteousness.*

Samuel awoke to what sounded like a lot of beeping and bright lights. His eyes roamed around as much as they could but he couldn't move his head at all. Something was blocking his range of movement. His ears came alive just then, although sounds were muffled. He began to hear orders being yelled and vital signs being read. He understood this was an orchestra of organized chaos. From what he could see, everyone was jumping and moving at a fast pace; too fast for his eyes to keep up with just one person. Someone, perhaps a nurse noticed he was awake and came over and started speaking to him. She told him not to move his head at all and that he was on his way to surgery. Sam's heart began to beat faster by the second, as thoughts of what happened earlier began to flood his memory.

He remembered the club, Club Fire. It should've been called Club Hell, for all it's costing him. He remembers the young man "Black" and the shots fired. He remembered going down but for some reason he just doesn't remember where he was hit. "My head, maybe that's why they don't want me to move it," he said to himself as they wheeled him towards the operating room. Sam started calculating his life in that instant. Did he do everything he was supposed to do? Would his kids be alright without him, especially his youngest? Did he update his will? Thoughts of death and not life consumed his mind until the lights in the O.R. became fuzzy and his eyes no longer wanted to obey his command to open once they closed.

The doctors worked furiously for hours repairing the injury to his neck. If the operation worked, he would be considered a miracle. The bullet not only did a lot of damage to his neck and shoulder, but it cut his jugular, so that he was bleeding profusely in and out of his body. The only thing the emergency room doctors could do was make sure he was stable enough and the bleeding controlled enough to go into surgery and let the surgeons do their job. The surgery lasted for over six hours. Repairing a jugular and all the damage done by a single bullet was no easy task. The doctors marveled at how much damage was done. The bullet hit the jugular vein and ricocheted into his left shoulder and lodged in his chest two inches away from his heart. The path the bullet took was confusing to the doctors but they were glad to have been able to save the life of one who saves lives himself.

Sam's eyes were still closed when he felt his body shaking and his name being yelled. "Am I dreaming?" he asked himself, eyes still closed. As Sam began to slowly open his eyes, it was to see he was in no dream, but a recovery room. He looked over to see the doctor standing over him smiling saying how successful the surgery was and that he was going to be all right. He still didn't understand. The doctor asked him not to speak or move his head but blink instead if he could hear him. Sam did as he was told. When asked about the pain, Sam blinked rapidly. It seemed like the whole left side of his body is in pain, especially his shoulder. The doctor patted his hand and told him things would be all right. He then looked across from him and yelled out some orders and left. All Sam could do was take a deep breath, and sleep.

*Acts 16:31 And they said, Believe on the Lord Jesus Christ, and thou shalt be saved, and thy house.*

Karen heard the news this morning that an officer got shot at the club last night. She didn't worry because she figured it wasn't Sam. She had overheard the street that the shooting occurred on over his radio, while they were on the phone the night before. The news said the officer's name was not released but his family was notified of the shooting.

Karen readies the plates of food for her son that she cooked last night. She smiles to herself in anticipation of the noise of smacking while eating. Shawn wasn't the one to eat with his mouth closed, even though she would fuss at him repeatedly for it. He would always tell her that good food deserved to be heard. She smiled harder thinking Sam would probably do the same thing once he got a taste of her food. She wondered when was the last time this father of four ate a home cooked meal like she prepared. She cooked turkey wings over rice, greens with fresh picked peppers and ham hocks, candy yams and a sweet potato pie so good it would have you questioning if she cooked it or God created it.

Karen heads to the hospital and at every red light she stopped and pulled out her phone checking for any missed calls from Sam. She even made a call to make sure the phone was on in case she forgot to pay the bill. She thought about the shooting but waved it off because she knew he didn't go to the club that night. "Maybe he's sleeping in today," she thought to herself as she pulled into the hospital garage parking. Karen checked her watch and seen it was too late for Sam to be sleeping in, as it was already one o clock in the afternoon. She knew he was an early riser, so that option was automatically ruled out. Karen had to shake herself, how could she hold the man to any schedule when he wasn't her man. She liked him to be though. She smiled at that thought. She was embarrassed for even thinking such a thing.

Karen knocks at the door before coming in. Shawn was a young man now and did not like being caught with "his pants down" since he was not able to clean himself at this time, a nurse had to do it. That was bad enough, but for her to walk in while it was being done was the shame of a lifetime that they agreed no one would find out about. She had a good laugh about that.

"Come in," he yelled from his bed.

"Hey baby. Hello boys," she greeted two of Shawn's friends as she entered the room.

"Oh please tell me there is real food in that bag with all that foil covering it," he said as he eyeballed the bag in her hands.

"If I'm not mistaken, I did say hey baby when I walked into the room. Now if the plate of food gets more respect than your mother, then I might just eat the food myself and see what that gets me!" she said with an eyebrow cocked right at Shawn.

He smiled. "Hey Ma, I'm so glad you're here. I was just telling Troy and Daniel about my nurse," he said as he smiled wider to show his sincerity.

"Hmm, did you tell them how beautiful she is?" she asked sarcastically. The boys snickered behind her because they saw the nurse for themselves.

"Very funny Ma, you're on your way to becoming a great comedienne," he shot back just as sarcastic.

"Why thank you son," she said as she pulled up a chair and the table near him for them to eat on. His friends from childhood chose to leave them to their "bonding" and go get some food themselves. Karen adjusted the bed for Shawn to sit him up as much as he could and attempted to feed him in which she was alerted quickly that he didn't need her to do that anymore.

"Uhh Ma, I do have a fully functional right arm," he said smiling.

"Ok ok, but can you cut with one hand too? Cause I would love to see that trick," she said sarcastically.

"You're just a bowl of sarcasm today huh? If I need help cutting, please believe Ma, I'm going to tell you."

The two ate in silence for several minutes before Shawn, being the young man that he is, decided to turn on the television. It was on the news channel he was watching last night to see if there was any leads in his case. None. Just as Karen was about to tell him to turn off the TV she heard what made her neck turn so quickly in cracked. The young lady was reading an update about the officer who got shot last night.

"After he murdered a young couple in cold blood in broad daylight on the street corner of Moncrief and Myrtle, Antoine Blounts, also known as Black to his friends went to Club Fire and went on a shooting spree inside the club, killing two more people and injuring seven. The officer's name that was shot is Officer Samuel Preston. The twenty one year veteran of the police force is in critical condition after the single shot that hit him in his neck. Nick, is there any more information you can give us about this case, like why Mr. Blounts did what he did?" she said as the story switched to another reporter standing outside the hospital.

"Dang Ma, you looking at this story like you know ole dude," he said watching her reaction.

"I do, and so should you being as that's the cop that saved your life," she said as she covered her food.

"What are you doing? Where are you going?" he questioned.

"I'm not going anywhere, I just lost my appetite," she said as she got up and walked to the window.

"Umm are you and this guy dating or something?" he asked.

"No Shawn, we're not dating. I just got the chance to get to know him and he's really a great guy and I hope he's going to be alright," she said worriedly.

"Well Ma, we are in the best hospital in the state and besides critical condition is what they put you in when you just get out of surgery. He's probably doing his thang right now," he said in between chews.

Karen smiled, "And what thang might that be Mr. know it all?" she asked as she walked back towards him.

"He probably talking cop stuff with his cop buddies, cracking cop jokes. He probably got the best nurses too. You know they get preferential treatment," he said as he shoveled another fork full of food into his mouth.

Karen laughed. She had to shake her head at her son's way of thinking. She hoped that Sam would be alright. She didn't have to wonder anymore why he didn't call; now she knew why. She wanted to see him but knew he would have limited visits because he was a cop. "His kids are probably with him now anyway," she thought to herself. She was deep in thought before Shawn intruded.

"Guess who found me AND called me today?" he asked.

"You have turkey gravy all over you," she said as she wiped his chin for him as he chewed on a drumstick. "Who called you, the president himself?" she asked jokingly.

"Stop yourself Whoopi Goldberg," he said un amused with her jokes.

"Ok ok so tell me already or do I have to wrestle the food away from you so you can tell me?" she said as she motioned like she was going to take his plate away.

Shawn's hand came down quickly to block the take away. He had to smile at that attempt, "Ya boy got skills now, I keep telling you I'm quick. Naw but for real, Terrance Mccloud called me today."

Karen stood still, her face stoic. Her ex husband and Shawn's father called? He hadn't spoken or seen Shawn in over fourteen years and now all of a sudden he calls.

"What the hell did he want?" she asked as she sat back down, frowning.

"He said he heard about the shooting and realized it was me and wanted to see how I was doing," he said as he quickly shoved another fork full of food into his mouth.

"Did you ask him why he hasn't BEEN seeing how you were doing? Why he waits till you nearly lose your life for him to call you? What kind of foolishness is that?" she said angrily.

"Uhhh I guess you don't want to hear anything else huh? He asked hesitantly.

"Oh there's more? Please do tell," she said, as her frown increased to an outright scowl.

"Well, he asked about you and he asked could he come see me."

"And what did you tell him?" Karen found it more difficult to stay in her seat but she would until she heard the answer.

"I told him yea," he said as he realized his plate was clean.

"Why would you tell him that? Why would you let that man come see you?" She sprang up out of her seat, no longer able to contain herself.

"Cause he's my dad Ma," he said emphatically.

"No! He's not," she answered.

"Ma!" he said looking at her, frowning now himself.

Karen had to catch herself, Shawn was right and she knew it. Terrance was his father, he might not have been a good one but it doesn't change the fact that he is. She looked at Shawn's face and knew this was something he wanted badly. He wanted and needed a man in his life. She just wished Terrance wasn't that man and Sam was.

"Alright Shawn, you're right he is your dad. So when is he coming to see you?" she asked as she sat back down.

"He said tomorrow, in the afternoon as soon as he gets off work," Shawn answered, watching her reaction. He knew and understood why she was upset, but he still wanted to see him. Even if it was the last time, he wanted to know his face.

"Alright, well that's good. I may not like it but he hasn't seen you in a while and vice versa so...it's good," she said as she remembered their last encounter. It wasn't a good one. "So what do you want me to do?"

"What do you mean?" He said as he rambled through the bag to find the pie. He couldn't help but to smile widely when he saw it.

Karen smiled too as she watched her son devour the two slices of pie she brought for him. "Do you want me to be here or do you want this to be just the two of you?" she asked.

"Well, I want to see the both of you here but I don't want you to be uncomfortable. I mean, I understand this dude

124

made life harder for us but it's something about him. I just want to see him," he said as he swallowed the last of the pie.

"I understand you wanting to see him. What I will do is just come at my regular time; if he's here then he's here. But if I miss him, then oh well," she said.

Shawn understood her meaning and smiled. She would make an attempt just for him. "You know what I was thinking Ma?" he asked as he watched her.

"What was you thinking boy?" she asked back.

"Your reaction to this cop getting shot was kind of strong. You sure ya'll two only cool or are ya'll warming up? He asked with a smile.

Karen's eyes got wide at the question and she couldn't control the blush creeping across her whole face. "Little boy, who told you it was alright to mind my business?" she asked as she got up and tried to clean up so Shawn wouldn't see the redness flooding her face. Too late.

"Well the way you blushing, it seems like things warming up. Just make sure things don't get too hot, know what I mean?" he asked rhetorically.

Karen turned around and found Shawn thoroughly amused at her. "I'm glad you find this funny but it's not and it's none of your business," she snapped.

"Come on now Ma. I've been the only dude in your conversation for over twelve years and now this dude gets shot and you looking like you could peel your skin off."

"First of all it's been over fourteen years and secondly, I've dated other guys so you were not the only man in my conversation during that time. Don't think you know everything about me little boy. Just because you didn't hear of a man or seen one, doesn't mean one didn't exist. And what the heck did you mean I looked like I wanted to peel my skin off?" She said as she twisted her neck like she told him.

"So you have been living a double life? How many men have you had in your life?" He asked bluntly ignoring the question.

"No I haven't been living a double life and that's none of your business. If I felt like their chances of having a stable relationship with me were shot, then I felt no reason to even bother to introduce them to you," she answered.

"What if I liked the dude?"

"That's exactly why I kept them away from you. I didn't want you liking somebody that had no future with us and we broke up and he up and left you high and dry with tears in your eyes," she answered.

"So this cop has a place in our life?" He asked as he looked in her eyes directly.

"This cop is a friend, nothing else. He's been there for me and helped me to understand things that I thought couldn't be understood. I think he is a wonderful and caring man. I don't know what the future holds but I wouldn't mind if he was in it." She smiled as she said that last part. Shawn smiled too; he would have to meet this one.

# CHAPTER 10

*James 5:14, 16 Is any sick among you? let him call for the elders of the church; and let them pray over him, anointing him with oil in the name of the Lord: (16)...the effectual fervent prayer of a righteous man avails much.*

Andrea didn't bother knocking on the door; she just slowly opened it instead and peeped inside. The room was dark and humid. Timothy has been going through his withdrawal for what seems like months but has only been two days. The guys from the church and even Pastor have been keeping their word. They have been there, around the clock since he first started his withdrawal. He had diarrhea, he was throwing up nothing because he hadn't eaten anything, sweating profusely but was shivering like he was in a deep freezer. The demons were playing havoc with his mind. He had scratches and whelps all over him like he was fighting all night and was on the losing end.

While the pastors and other members were laying hands and praying, Andrea was also praying. She walked around the house for hours praying in tongues, binding and loosing. She did whatever she thought was necessary in order to break and keep this curse away from her son. She was dedicated to him, and as far as she was concerned, there was no turning back.

When his symptoms first started, the guys removed the carpet out of the room because they knew what to expect. Timothy had no control over his body; it functioned in its own way. He couldn't hold anything in or down. The pain from the cramps and withdrawal made him hallucinate but his resolve was to finish this. Timothy was not about to be back on that block. He didn't care if this killed him; he wasn't going back. Sometimes they would go in his room and he would be naked on the floor screaming, other times it was to find him in the bed moaning what could not be understood.

The pastor tried his best to explain in a spiritual manner the process of withdrawal to Andrea, trying to keep her hope in her son and not attention to the pain.

"Andrea I know it's hard seeing your child go through this, but when he comes out it'll be worth it," he said.

"It's very hard. I sometimes wonder if it's worth it; all the pain, the cramps, the diarrhea, the wounds. I mean is it really worth it?" she asked.

"It's worth it. I think you're looking at this in the wrong way. Let me show you a different way," he said as he sat down at the kitchen table.

Andrea joined him. "Please do," she said as she sat back to listen.

"It's like a woman giving birth, you want to help the pain but you can't. But you know what's coming out of her will make the difference. It's the same way with Timothy. You look at it as his body is punishing him for not giving it the drugs. I look at it as the pain he is going through is the body

128

ridding itself of the residual. It's going to take a lot because he has taken a lot. He's been taking drugs for years yet his body is going to get rid of the yearn and desire that was there for years in a few days," he explained.

"I understand what you're saying, but as a mother..." she didn't finish; she couldn't finish. The tears came streaming down her eyes.

"As a mother keep doing what you're doing. As a mother, you can't stop or help in the process because you'll be hindering his deliverance and I know you don't want that," he said compassionately.

"I don't want to hinder but I do want to help!" she exclaimed, now at the edge of her chair.

"You are helping. You're doing the most important part. You're praying. It's you that's keeping him strengthened. If you lose strength, so does he."

The tears seemed to fall in slow motion out of Andrea's eyes. She understood everything the Pastor was saying but wanted so badly to see and hold her child, even if for five minutes. She wanted to tell him things would be better, that the pain wouldn't last. She wanted him to hear her voice, but she knew she had to step back and allow Tim to hear the voice of God for himself.

Andrea had been so focused on Tim and his process that she paid no attention to her other kids, and they came to find out why! Justine was first through the door. She was just about to speak when she noticed the pastor and looked at her mother and seen the tears. The assumptions started to fly immediately.

"What are you crying for Mother? Did you not know he was going to do this?" she asked smugly.

"What are you talking about Justine and don't you ever come in my house again and not speak to my guests. I raised you better than that," Andrea said.

"Oh I'm sorry, hello Pastor," she said sarcastically. "Maybe you should've told my mother to give up on that degenerate son of hers." she remarked.

"You shut your stupid mouth girl. You have no idea what we are talking about. You just walk into my house assuming with your conceited self cause you think you know everything when you don't know squat!" By this time Andrea was hot. She stood up and the only thing blocking her from getting to Justine was Pastor. He had to jump in or she would jump him!

"Ladies, ladies please calm down. This isn't helping the situation any," he said being the mediator.

"What did he steal now? Oh wait, let me guess," she said as she feigned thinking, "He broke into your room and you don't know how. And stole all your money because you're not smart enough to put it in a bank!" she screamed.

"Girl the ONLY reason you still standing is because of Pastor and the ONLY reason I ain't cussed you out yet is because of Pastor. You so foolish but I'm going to tell you this. Put my keys on the table walk out and keep it moving. Do your thing and don't worry about me and mines. You are no longer welcomed in my house!" She said hotly.

"Whatever! I don't know why you're trying to be so difficult, acting as if it's my fault. Timothy did it, not me," she said defensively.

"Timothy did what Justine? What are you talking about?"

"I'm talking about whatever you're crying about, that's what!" she said.

"Justine, you're assuming something is wrong when nothing really is," the pastor interjected.

"Oh well, if nothing is really wrong, then where is Tim?" she asked.

"Tim's in the back room you idiot!" Andrea yelled.

"You really shouldn't judge your brother because as far as I see, you're no better yourself Justine," the pastor was getting angry now.

"Excuse you!!" she said in disbelief. "You don't even know me Pastor to even speak to me in such a manner. How dare you? I am far better than that crack head. I don't do drugs. I am a faithful tither, as if you didn't already know that and I give an offering, a big one. I don't go out nor drink nor curse. I am much better than that thing you call my brother." She said pointedly.

"Ok I'll give you that. You do all of those things and that's good, but God doesn't look at the finances, he looks at the heart. Your heart is filthy. It's what comes out of a man that defiles." He said plainly.

"I am not defiled Pastor. And since God doesn't look at finances, guess you won't be needing mine any longer," she said as she looked the pastor up and down.

"I don't rely on what man does, but every word out of the mouth of God," he rebutted.

"If I was you, I'd try to keep every member I get. Your church isn't exactly big now is it? Can you afford to lose any of us?" she said twisting her face in all sorts of pointless expressions.

The pastor laughed. "The church doesn't belong to man, but to God. I didn't bring you in, so I can't stop you from leaving. I know this Justine, when one moves; God is replacing or has already replaced that person with more. So I'm not worried about who leaves or stays, that's Gods problem," he said as he smiled.

"You have an answer for everything, don't you Pastor?" she asked

"You've gone too far little girl. Go home to your cheating husband, go home and be a mother to that little boy that would rather wear one of your dresses than be the man he was created to be," Andrea said, creeping around the pastor.

"My son is more of a man than Tim will ever be and at least my husband is alive. And I don't have to use my son to try to fill his place," she said. The words came out so fast that she didn't have the time to think about what she was saying. Immediately she regretted what she said.

Andrea's tears came as the floodgates opened. She couldn't believe her own child said that. For some reason she was calm, and she would stay that way.

"Ok Justine, you said it. Are you happy? Did that make you feel good? Well I'm glad it's all out in the open and there's no more hiding. As I said, leave my keys on the table and keep it moving. I'm committed to Timothy. I love him; he's my son. You don't understand that then oh well that's not my concern. But you are no longer welcomed here. Don't call me, don't write me, and don't send anyone to find out about me. You think you know everything, all right Justine.

You handle you and your family and I'm going to handle mine." She said as she began to walk away.

"Mom, why can't you just see that I love you and I'm hurt too? Timothy hurt me too, I put my trust in that boy," she said.

"The bible says put your trust in no flesh. That's not Tim's fault, that's yours," she said still walking down the hall.

"Apologize Justine," the pastor practically begged her.

"Pastor I appreciate you, but that's not her character. People who know everything won't apologize for what they didn't know," she said as she just stood in the hallway.

"Fine Mother, you've made your bed now lay in it. Don't call me when he messes up again because all you're going to hear is I told you so," she said defiantly. Pride was keeping the apology from her lips. An apology that she wanted to give but couldn't. After all, she knew it all. Didn't she?

"Justine, I wouldn't call you if I was in hell and you had the only bucket of water," Andrea said smiling just as defiantly as Justine was looking.

Justine was leaving just as Kevin was pulling up. He noticed how she slammed the door as she left and knew not to speak or he too might lose his head. He knocked on the door and was surprised to see the Pastor there. Instead of thinking the way Justine did, Kevin went in a totally different direction.

"Oh Jesus, he's dead isn't he?" He asked grabbing the pastor's lapels.

"Who's dead?" The pastor asked as Andrea threw her hands up in the air.

"Timothy," he answered now looking at his mother.

"No boy, no one is dead. Timothy is fine, he's going through detox but he's fine. Thanks for asking. What the hell do you want?" She asked with her hands on her hips, looking quite aggravated.

"Uh, I came to check on you since I haven't heard from you in a minute Ma," he said surprised by her question.

"I'm fine as you can see," she said turning herself around in a full circle for Kevin to see. "Now please leave. Go hang with your friends like you usually do. When did I ASK you to come see me? Go chill with one of your hoochie mama's that you would stand me up for. What? You ain't got no bowling tonight? Maybe you should go check and make sure. Just get out," Andrea was past the point of aggravation. She was through with the both of them. She wished Simone was here instead of in Germany. She might have been the second youngest but she was definitely the wisest. Justine couldn't stand her because in no way could she act like she was better in front of Simone. She didn't mind putting you on front street and then will beat you down just because. Out of five kids, she only liked two. That's the way they wanted it.

The next few days came and went without a hitch. Timothy was beginning to look human again and was actually eating and able to keep it down. Andrea changed the locks on all her doors and changed her cell and house phone numbers. If she could move, she would. The pastor was there every day helping her not only with Tim but with her other kids as well. He didn't want her holding onto what Justine said. He

134

didn't want her living with unforgiveness in her heart. So he ministered to her as well as to Timothy.

By the time the week ended, Timothy was able to bathe himself and eat semi normal food. He knew and understood just what happened and was happy it was over. Now for the hard part, walking in his newness.

"Hey cutie," Andrea said as she entered his room.

"Hey Ma, how are you?" He asked.

"I'm good, I'm about to go in this kitchen and cook us up a feast," she said excitedly.

"Why you cooking a lot of food? You expecting guests?" he asked.

"Nope, just gotta put meat on them bones son. You look like a bird that just escaped through the bars of a locked cage," she said laughing.

Tim smiled. He hasn't been able to do that in a week. It felt good to see his mother laughing. He was still too weak to laugh as hard as she was laughing but he smiled as hard as he could.

*Psalms 147:3* *He healeth the broken in heart, and bindeth up their wounds.*

Karen stood still on a sixth floor of the hospital. She hadn't seen Terrance in twelve years but he hadn't seen Shawn in over fourteen. The last time they met, she wasn't working yet and in desperate need of money. He told her he would give it to her but at the cost of her self-respect. Of course he wanted to sleep with her, she wanted it too until she walked in and found out his boy wanted in on the action. It was him who told the friend to pay her because "he wasn't paying for any prostitutes".

She was devastated and ashamed. Is that what he seen her as? She was his ex wife and the mother of his child; did he have ANY respect for her? For Shawn? Karen left that day without the money but with confidence. She left knowing she would make it. She didn't know how but she knew she was going to make it.

She looked like a statue standing there in the middle of the floor with a plate of food in her hands. The butterflies turned into eagles in her stomach. She never forgot, would she ever? God forgave her, could she forgive him? The thoughts swam around in her head like synchronize swimmers. As she began to walk towards the door, nurses stopped and asked if she was alright. Apparently, her mind started walking before her feet did. She smiled and with a little coercion, they moved. She stood in front of Shawn's door and listened. She wanted to hear what he was saying, what he was lying about. She couldn't hear anything. So she opened the door.

Terrance stood there watching the door open slowly. There she was, beautiful, as ever yet she looked upset to see him. He smiled at her to comfort her but she barely cracked her lips to speak as she brushed past him to pull up the chair and table to Shawn so he could eat. She sat the plate down and unwrapped it for him, then sat down next to him and watched him say his grace and dig into the meal.

"Dang it Karen, none for me? Terrance said rubbing his stomach.

"Dang it? Where did that come from?" she asked.

"Oh I don't swear anymore, a lot of things have changed about this old man Karen," he said smiling.

"I see. So tell me what else has changed" she inquired.

"I stopped drinking and doing drugs and I definitely stopped going out," he said.

"Mmm, your women must hate that," she said with her brows raised.

"I gave them up too. Look Karen, I'm sorry about the things I've done and said to you..." he said as she raised her hand to cut him off.

"This isn't about me, it's about Shawn. That's why you're here right?" she asked.

"Well of course I am," he answered.

"There will be other opportunities to speak to me, if that is what you want. Right now your attention should be on your son and him alone. At least while you're here," she said as she smiled.

He understood her meaning. She will not discuss the past in front of Shawn at this time. Karen looked really good to him. She's done well without him but he couldn't help but to wonder if there was anybody in her life and if not, did he have a chance. He knew he would have to be patient and see if forgiveness was possible with her. At least for right now, she was giving him more than he deserved.

Karen sat there and watched Terrance. He was a little older but he still looked good. He was still doing construction, she could tell by his hands. He looked as nervous as he probably was feeling but she wasn't nervous surprisingly. She just sat there and listened to the conversation between him and Shawn. He actually sounded like a changed man, he sounded more mature.

She eyeballed him from head to toe. He had a great body before but it looks even better now. His smile was still mesmerizing but yet she was immune to it. She smiled at his humor as he told a joke. She choked at his bluntness in talking about the nurses. She watched the muscles in his chest move under the hideous plaid shirt he wore. Karen had to take a deep breath; it's been a while since she's been with a man. The one thing she could give Terrance was that he was definitely all man. She watched his every move as he reached up and turned on the TV for Shawn. She watched the stretch of the muscles in his back and wished she could touch the cheeks of his buttocks before Shawn intruded upon her lustful thoughts.

"Ma, did you hear about your friend?" he asked.

"What friend baby?" she asked.

"Your officer friend, he'll be going through physical therapy with me," he said.

That caught her off guard, she wasn't expecting that. Had she forgotten about Sam that quickly? "How did you hear about this?" she asked.

"The nurses, they are the nosiest women on the planet. And it seems like they got major crushes on ya boy. You better make your presence known," he said sideways.

"Little boy, didn't we have this conversation the other day?" She asked shyly, trying not to let Terrance know her business.

"Ma, he is your friend. Have you seen him yet? Did you go visit him at all?" He asked shoving the last piece of cornbread in his mouth.

"Actually no, I just figured I wouldn't intrude on his time with his family. I mean this has been a traumatic time for him and for them," she said.

"Aww Ma, what kind of girlfriend are you?" He said smiling.

"I am **NOT** his *GIRLFRIEND*!!!" she yelled.

"Ok then what kind of friend are you? My friends came and seen me in spite of you. So you mean you can't go see this dude cause his family is there? I'm sure his other friends don't feel that way and I'm *dern* sure he don't feel *that* way!" He said as he took every excuse away on why she couldn't or wouldn't go see Sam.

Karen couldn't believe how bad her son made her feel. She spent all the time in the world thinking of Sam but no time visiting him. She didn't know how his family felt because she never tried to find out. She made up in her mind she would go see if she could pay him a visit after she left Shawn. Right now, Terrance had her undivided attention.

"So I hear you're a big time nurse Karen," Terrance said as he pulled the chair up next to her.

"Not big time, but I must say I'm a darn good nurse" she said confidently.

"You were always good at everything you did so that doesn't surprise me," he said.

"Thank you" she said leaning to the side to get a full view of his face. That's the first compliment he's given her in a very long time.

"No need to thank me, at least not for the truth. Now for that handsome young man lying on that bed, you can thank me," he said jokingly.

Karen never would have thought in a million years that she could stay much less sit in the same room as her ex-husband and baby daddy and not try to kill him. But here they were joking and laughing with each other like old friends. Shawn might be blind in one eye, but he was able to see clearly that something wonderful could happen.

"Terrance you lost your mind, Shawn looks and acts just like me. You ain't had nothing to do with that!" She said as she smiled.

"I beg to differ, he has my tenacity and he may favor you but he has my features," he rebutted. As he continued speaking, Karen sat in disbelief. She still couldn't believe that not only were they having a decent conversation, but also she was laughing and having a good time with him. She really was enjoying herself with her son's father slash ex-husband. He was cruel and manipulating in their marriage, but as she sat there and watched him, that wasn't the man she was seeing. He was verbally abusive and an adulterer but yet he sat here complimenting her and acting faithful. She smiled; she had to snap herself back to reality. Just because he's changed doesn't mean he's changed for her.

Karen heard her phone go off in her purse that was sitting on the floor beside her. As Terrance and Shawn spoke about sports and cars, she read the message on her phone. Something jumped inside of her when she read ROOM 602 IN CASE YOU DIDN'T KNOW. Sam wanted to see her. She was so caught up in how good Terrance looked that she forgot how great Sam was. So she jumped up and grabbed her purse and told Shawn she would see him tomorrow. She looked at Terrance and shook his hand, which was as close as she was willing to get. She wished him well, told him it was nice seeing him again and she left and headed down the hall and around the corner to Sam's room.

She heard the voice of a younger man in the room and knew he had company but she knocked anyway. Even if it was just to say hi and bye, she wanted to see him. Sam turned his head and saw her standing in his doorway and couldn't help but to flash the biggest smile he had in his arsenal. He was not just happy to see her but ecstatic. She looked absolutely beautiful to him and it showed. His son stood there staring at the stranger at the door wondering, who was this woman that made his father smile so wide? He watched her as she walked in smiling just as widely herself. He watched as she gently touched his father's hand and watched as his father grabbed hers. The atmosphere change was almost immediate but he was glad to see the shift.

"Hello there Mr. Policeman," she said smiling down at him.

"I'm so glad you're here. How have you been? How's Shawn?" he asked.

"Whoa slow down Sam. How are **you** doing?" She asked as she noticed, they were still holding hands.

"I was good, but I'm better now," he said smiling; hoping she understood he meant it was because of her that he was doing better. "How's Shawn?" He asked.

"He's doing great, he's with his father right now," she said.

"Wow, his father actually showed up. That's great," he said.

"Yes it is. They have a lot of catching up to do, fourteen years worth," she said, still holding his hand.

His son smiled, he was actually forgotten. That wouldn't last for long!

"Umm hello there, I'm Matthew" he said as he approached Karen with his hand ready to shake hers. She was startled as she forgot she heard the voice of another in the room but Sam commanded her attention in that way.

"Hello Matthew, I apologize for not speaking before. I'm Karen, a friend of your father's," she said, shaking his hand.

"How did you know he was my father? Did he show you that potty picture of me?" He asked seriously.

"Umm no Matthew, he didn't show me that picture, but I'm going to insist he does now. You are the spitting image of him, that's how I knew you were his son" she said as she looked back at Sam.

Sam laid there smiling at her. He wanted to see how she would interact with his children and no better time than the present.

"Matt you gave yourself away son, now I gotta show her that picture," he said smiling at Matthew.

"Oh no you don't, I'm surprised you didn't already because that seems to be the first picture you show off of me," he said to his father. Then turning back to face Karen, he said, "It's not the best picture of me."

"No it's not but it sure is one of the funniest I have of you," he said laughing.

Karen was nervous when Matthew came forward and introduced himself, but he made her feel comfortable with his humor and easy mannerisms. She realized he was just like Sam in so many ways. He was the carefree type, yet he had a serious side. The three of them sat and talked for hours. She learned so much more about Sam that she didn't know. Simple stuff, stuff he didn't like and what he loved. She listened as they spoke about everything from food to sports. She learned all of his kids had biblical names and what they stood for. She learned a lot about Matthew too. He was going to school to be an electrical engineer but had his minor in religion. He was the most challenging one to raise as he did that by himself after the death of his wife, but the young man was responsible and respectful.

Karen laughed so hard as father and son began cracking jokes on each other. Her side began to cramp and hurt as the tears rolled down her cheeks. She was laughing so hard that both the men looked at her and began laughing at her. Karen was enjoying herself so much that she for once forgot about Shawn and she definitely forgot about Terrance. She was in a different place and time. When Matthew left, she stayed with Sam. She sat right next to his bed and watched TV with him and talked to him until he fell asleep. She looked at him as he slept and knew she could fall in love with this man. She held his hands until his nurse came in to do her rounds. He didn't want her to leave but visiting hours were over hours ago but the nurses let him have the extra time as long as his guests didn't disturb the other patients.

He watched as she picked up her purse to get ready to leave. He didn't want her to go but knew she had to.

"So Karen MCCloud, when will I see you again? That home cooked meal would sure come in handy right about now," he said licking his lips.

"I will bring you a plate tomorrow Samuel Preston. I'm sorry it took me so long to come see you. I thought with everything that happened that you would just want to see your family," she explained.

"Nope, they made me feel ok but they were so sad and worried. I needed someone that would make me feel great and that's what you did when I seen you tonight. Thank you for coming." He said as he watched her.

"I don't know where this is going but I intend on enjoying the ride," she said as she slung the purse on her shoulder.

"That makes two of us, but I must say I'm enjoying the ride thus far," he said as he smiled sweetly at her.

"Me too Sam, me too. Well get some sleep and I'll see you tomorrow," she said as she walked out. She was in another world altogether. She didn't understand what was going on but she wanted it to happen and she was going to do just what she told Sam, she was going to enjoy the ride. She touched the door as she passed by Shawn's room and said a little prayer of protection as she continued towards the elevators. Karen was surprised by all the things that was happening in one day. So much so that she looked forward to what would happen the next day. She drove home in

144

anticipation of cooking for the two men of her life, one she loved dearly and one that she knew she could fall in love with. What surprised her most was not the fact that he was someone she could fall in love with, it was the fact that he was someone she WANTED to fall in love with. Karen smiled herself to sleep, Sam was there waiting for her.

# CHAPTER 11

*Matthew 7:15 Beware of false prophets, which come to you in sheep's clothing, but inwardly they are ravening wolves.*

Tyrone has been on top of the world and wished Travis was there to see it so he could laugh in his face. The god Tyrone was serving was doing a powerful thing in his life while the God Travis was serving was doing absolutely nothing, or so he thought. Tyrone smiled at his reflection in the mirror, he looked good and that was an understatement. He wore a black Armani suit with a tan shirt and a tan tie that matched the handkerchief that was in his top left pocket. He sported a goatee but no moustache and had somewhat of a beard but it was kept really close. He kept his haircut and faded but still had enough to show the world his "good hair" he got from his grandmother. His teeth were white and straight, and his eyes were light brown yet not quite hazel but nonetheless mesmerizing.

Tyrone took pride in his looks. He grew up knowing he looked good. He was told he couldn't dress like everybody else or it would take away from his looks. That was unacceptable to him. He lived and felt like he was royalty so he had to act the part. Forget the dreads and gold or platinum teeth; forget the sagging pants and wife beaters. Yea he had Jordan's and Timberland boots but even when he wore them, he wore them in class. He learned how to dress like the world but be distinguished from the rest of the world.

He kept his body in tiptop condition. He only ate natural foods and kept water running through him. He rarely ate red meat more than twice a year and pork was out of the question. He exercised six days a week and rested one. His neck made you think twice if you ever thought about choking him. His biceps looked as if every shirt he wore, they would burst through. He made sure that men knew that the body was the temple and in order for God to dwell in that temple, it had to be well taken care of. Who would want to dwell in a run down, dilapidated temple? He would ask them. Every man he came in contact with left his presence with a workout goal in mind. He was so convincing and had the ability to draw people unto God, but that wasn't his intentions.

Whenever men looked at him, they were jealous. If they were straight, they wanted to be him. If they were gay, they wanted to be with him. The women were no different; they wanted to be his wife, his girl on the side or whatever they could be. They didn't care that he was a "man of God". He invoked lustfulness in the people wherever he went. He preached with passion and fervency and would even preach against his own lifestyle but somehow managed to be able to separate word from deed.

His rule to sleeping with men was easy; they had to have a lot to lose. He slept with other prominent preachers, businessmen, and of course, other married men. He stayed away from single men for obvious reasons. Tonight he was in Washington D.C., scheduled the last night to preach, but this was his night to relax and survey the field. He may not have been the speaker but he was definitely in the limelight. People paid to come see and hear him and he knew this. He was going to be the closer for the conference and the title he was going to preach on was "Men of God, Come out of Hiding". His wife was home with his two boys so he was free to do as he pleased.

Tyrone showed up early to the conference, as was his nature to do. He didn't believe in being late to nothing, even if he wasn't scheduled to minister. He was the type that came early and stayed late. He didn't mind rolling up his sleeves and getting dirty, that's what kept everyone off guard. When it came to ministry-God worked through Tyrone in a very powerful way. No one would suspect a thing because he was all about the people. All about helping and ministering to the people. He was quick to take off his jacket and tie and get muddy if the occasion called for it. He was handsome, powerful, humble and a laborer. He was everything that the people wanted; yet none of what God wanted. He had engagements booked out a year in advance. He was basically the poster boy for Christianity. It appears that since he got saved, he has been running hard and on fire for God. Looks are dangerously deceiving.

Tyrone blinded people by the things he did. He made sure to give huge offerings to let everyone know he's blessed. People watched everything he did, but yet they didn't know who labored among them. They looked to the things he had externally, the wife, cars, houses, money etc. but no one paid any attention to what was going on internally. If someone would just listen, they would hear that voice telling them to "BEWARE OF WOLF IN SHEEP'S CLOTHING". No one was listening so he continued to climb to the top of the Church like King Kong.

As Tyrone stepped out of his limo, it was to find the conference in a bit of confusion. The speaker for that night cancelled at the last minute due to a death in his immediate family. Someone had to take his place, but whom? Who else?

"Minister Tyrone Baxter," yelled the MC, another prominent Pastor. "How are you sir?" He asked with his hand outstretched to shake Tyrone's.

"Doing well man of God," Tyrone said as he shook the Pastor's hand.

"Good, good. I trust that your accommodations have been good thus far," he stated but had the look of a question.

"Oh yes, the accommodations have been more than excellent. Thank you Pastor. Everything set for tonight?" He asked.

"Minister Baxter, the headlining preacher had to pull out due to a death and I'm left with an empty spot on the first night of this conference. You know the first night sets the tempo for the rest of the conference. I haven't been able to really sit down and gather my thoughts together to get a word for me to preach tonight so I'm going to have to wing it up there. I'm not sure what else to do, I'm emceeing and preaching tomorrow night. Now I have to switch everything around. What a mess!" He explained.

"Pastor I'm not sure if you're in a mess or an opportunity," Tyrone said stopping to face the Pastor.

"What do you mean?" He asked curiously as he too stopped.

"Well I preach on Friday, that means I can preach tonight and still have time to get another word together for Friday.

I can just preach Friday's message tonight and that way you don't have to wear so many hats." He said as he smiled at his own suggestion.

"That's a great idea Minister Baxter, but are you sure you don't mind? I will make sure that you are well taken care of for preaching both nights," he said slapping Tyrone on the back as they began to walk again.

"I'm sure and I'm not doing this for the money. God has given me a word and I'm available. Why not do the work HE called me to do?" He asked.

"Minister, I'm sure glad you're here. You're more than a preacher, young man you're a lifesaver. Thank you. I must call your Bishop and tell him how much I appreciate the ministry gift he sent me for this conference. You're going to impact these men all over Washington D.C. tonight and I'm getting excited just thinking about it. I'll have your armor bearer show you to your seat. Anything that you need or want, don't you dare hesitate to ask me for it." He said.

"I promise sir, I'm already well taken care of. I'm excited as well because God gave me such a revealing word for the men in this season. It's basically just bubbling up in me," he said.

"No need to explain son. I know the feeling, that's why I didn't want to preach twice because the word God gave me is going to have me preaching like a mad man," he said laughing.

"Pastor, the last time I seen you, you were preaching like a mad man. I loved every moment of it and I'm looking forward to hearing the word God put in your belly. I know I will learn plenty from you this week," he said in mock humility.

"Son, I'm absolutely positive that the old will learn from the young at this conference. You go ahead and get yourself together to deliver that bubbling word you got in your belly. I need to get some last minute things done. I'll meet you in the pulpit when I'm finished," he said as he shook Tyrone's hand in parting.

As the conference started, Tyrone was introduced and performed beyond the expectations of everybody. Everything flowed like water over rocks, nothing disturbing the move of God. Tyrone preached so hard, he had to take off his jacket and tie. Sweat beaded up on his head but couldn't fall because someone was there wiping it ever so often. He had the men in a literal trance. His preaching style and words used made every man in the place wish to be as close to God as he was.

Men were coming forth to be healed and saved. Men were coming forth to put their past behind them at the altar. Men were coming forth to become better parents and kings in society. His words stirred the emotions of men that otherwise wouldn't move. The pastor and the rest of the ministers looked in amazement at the amount of men that came forward wanting and begging for prayer. Men of all ages were flocking to Tyrone like he was Jesus, just to touch some part of him. The Pastor just smiled and shook his head, offering should be absolutely fantastic tonight. He knew that because of Tyrone, the conference was a guaranteed success.

Tyrone knew it too. He smiled as he stood back and surveyed his work. He shook his head in content, he was happy with his performance. He wanted to make a statement and as he watched the men falling over each other to get to him for prayer, he knew he made that statement. It was as loud and as clear as you can get. His statement was I AM THE MAN!

*Revelation 21:4 And God shall wipe away all tears from their eyes; and there shall be no more death, neither sorrow, nor crying, neither shall there be any more pain: for the former things are passed away.*

It's been two years since Sondra has seen Michael. Life was hard but much better without him. Sondra's father died three months prior, he had a heart attack while preaching one Sunday morning. It devastated Sondra because it seems like the last months of his life were the best months of hers. God really healed and developed their relationship so much that even her mother saw the difference. They were close before, but this closeness was more spiritual than it was natural and she cherished every moment spent in it. Sondra's heart was slowly being healed as the days went by. She realized this as she entered the third month of his death. The reality of it became more tolerable than at first. She relished in the fact that he passed away doing what he loved best, saving souls.

Timothy has been free and sober for several months now and is even back to work. His body was beginning to take the shape of the fit young man he once was because of all the work he's been putting into the gym. He hasn't felt this good in years, and he intended on staying that way. Before he came off of the drugs, he was like one hundred and twenty pounds soaking wet, now he was more like two hundred and twenty pounds. His face was filled out and all the women took notice at the work the Lord did in him. No woman wanted to be with a crack head but maybe they would want to be with an ex addict who was now a responsible young man.

The pastor introduced him to Sondra several months ago, when he first started going to the gym. He wasn't in the best shape and was fresh off of withdrawal. She wasn't interested then, but lately she's been showing signs that she might be. Timothy has been doing a lot of work in the community and out. He's been working on houses and churches as well businesses. He lay whatever type of floor you wanted and if you allowed his creativity to flow, he'll make you wish you had more work for him to do.

Timothy always wanted to do the floors of his own church. He wanted to bless the pastor with the work but the pastor had already hired some guy to do the work. The work was horrible to Tim, it was sloppy and the tiles were mismatched. Even the pastor saw the obvious and not so obvious mistakes the man did. The Pastor was very upset, after all, this was work he was paying for. All he wanted to do was to add to the church, this guy was taking away from it. The worker and the pastor had words one night before service and the guy left and told him he wasn't going to finish the work. This was Timothy's chance to give back to a man that had supported and given him so much more.

"Hey Pastor" he said smiling.

"There's my son!" He said as he flashed a tired smile. "You know I adopted you right?" He asked jokingly.

"I'm glad you did. You're the only father I've always known," he said seriously.

"Walk with me" he said, still looking down at the floor "What you doing here so early? Something on your mind?" He asked.

"Actually yea, something is on my mind," Timothy said.

"Well wassup, spit it out," Pastor said as he turned and looked at him.

"I saw how these floors are and I want to help. I can help," he said looking at the floors himself.

"I don't know Tim, I don't know if these floors can be helped. I called myself trying to improve the look, trying to give it more appeal and look, I just messed it up instead," he said pointing to the floor.

"It can be fixed, just let me fix it. I do harder work than this on a daily basis, let me do what I do," he said trying to convince the Pastor.

"Tim I would love to but I spent so much money getting the guy to do this mess that I don't think I have enough to pay you. Matter of fact I know I don't have enough to pay you. And we have conferences coming up; one after another starting next month."

"First of all, this isn't even going to take me a week to do. Secondly Pastor, I didn't ask you for one red cent. This is something I'm doing because this is my home. I'm supposed to leave it like this when I know I can fix it? All I'm asking is you let me do it. When I'm done doing my work, I can come straight here and start on the floors. You'll still be here, I'm not asking to do anything outside of your time frame and I will still get it done in a week; I'm sure you're going to love it," Timothy said.

"Alright Tim, I can't see it getting any worse. So when can you start?" he asked.

"I'll be here tomorrow around three," he answered.

"What about the tiles?" Pastor asked.

"I own my own business, you keep forgetting that. I have my own tiles, I'll just use what I have," he answered again.

"Alright Tim, the floors are all yours, just please don't disappoint me. I don't think I could take it right now," he said as they walked into his office.

"Come on Pastor, I'm putting my name and reputation on the line. I'm not in the business of disappointing, just satisfying people," he said with a smile.

"You sound like a commercial," the pastor laughed. He was beginning to relax, he knew Timothy took great pride in his work and wasn't worried about it any longer, but he was curious about his love life. "So are you dating Sondra yet?" He asked curiously.

"Oh it's nothing like that Pastor," he said smiling widely, "I'm interested but I'm not sure if she is. I'm just trying to take it one day at a time especially since her father's death."

"yea, we lost a wonderful man there. He was such a good friend, and outside of God, he was the best friend a man could have. I miss him dearly. But have you even asked the girl for her number?" He questioned.

"No not yet, I'm just taking my time that's all," he stated.

"Well boy how much time you think you got? She's a beautiful young woman. There are a lot of guys that have their eyes on her; you're the best candidate. You better make your move before the next man does!" He advised.

"You're right, I'll ask her tonight then," he said shaking his head in agreement.

"Good, that's what I'm talking about. Now go start prayer," he said pointing to the sanctuary.

"What???" Timothy questioned in surprise.

"It's time you start walking in the things of God. You don't hang around me for no reason. God is ready to use you to free up some captives. Now go out there and start prayer. When the other deacons get here you can pass the microphone to one of them, but I want you to start it off. Your role in the church is going to get bigger and bigger, so you better be prepared, now go start prayer!" The pastor said smiling as Timothy left his office hesitantly.

Timothy worried about what he was going to say during prayer. His prayer time was spent talking and listening to God, not the way these men was calling down fire. Timothy grabbed the mic nervously but when he opened his mouth, the words came out of nowhere and the fire was ignited.

Sondra entered the sanctuary to find Timothy praying. She was pleasantly surprised and elated all at the same time. It was time for him to step into his calling she thought to herself. She sat down in her usual seat in hopes that he would notice her and come sit next to her when he was done. She liked him and was hoping the feeling was mutual. She couldn't really focus on praying as she stared at his six foot two frame pacing the floor by the altar admonishing people to live by the spirit and not the flesh.

She couldn't help but to smile as he never once opened his eyes until one of the other deacons approached to pray as well. He looked as if the microphone was a hot potato when he passed it with all quickness to the awaiting deacon. He noticed her as he walked away from the altar and smiled at her and she smiled back. She waved him over to her.

"Hey there," he said greeting her.

"Hey yourself preacher," she said smiling.

"Oh you got jokes huh?" he asked smiling back at her.

"I was wondering where you were sitting tonight," she asked shyly.

"I can sit next to you," he said boldly.

"I would like that," she said looking away.

"Let me get my bible, I'll be right back. Oh maybe we can study together over the phone," he said nonchalantly.

"I think that's something we can do," she said, this time looking at him.

"Great, I'll be right back," he said as he went and got his bible. He didn't notice his mother smiling in the back watching them. She knew Sondra was a good girl and he was a good boy. She knew they were right for each other. She looked to Heaven just to let God know, it's HIS Will not hers.

*1 Peter 3:15 But sanctify the Lord God in your hearts: and be ready always to give an answer to every man that asketh you a reason of the hope that is in you with meekness and fear:*

"You're going down for life Fred, that or the death penalty," the detective yelled.

"For what, what proof do you have that I killed that man?" Fred said calmly.

"Fred, you know what? Let's start this thing all over. You came here to talk, so let's talk. That guy had a baby on the way. He was already a father of two. Don't you have kids man?" The detective asked as he sat down next to Fred.

"Yea I got kids," he answered.

"How many you got Fred?" The detective asked.

"I got three that I know about," he answered.

"So how do you think your baby mamas would feel if someone gunned you down just because you said their girl was good looking?" The detective said leaning into the young man. "Do you see how stupid that was? And you did it right in front of a camera. Your face is blatant on there, you want to see it?" The detective asked. Fred shook his head yes, if what the detective was saying was true then his mind was already made up as to what his next move would be. It's called self-preservation.

The Detectives wheeled a TV into the interview room and put the DVD into the player. They let the DVD play until it came to the two men arguing and the one shooting the other point blank in his head, killing him instantly. He saw his face and knew as his head slumped, it was over for him but he had an ace up his sleeve.

"Tell me what happened Fred, tell me the truth," the detective said calmly.

"How bad do you want Paul James?" He asked the detective.

The two detectives looked at each other then back at the young man sitting in the seat. They wanted Paul badly, but how bad?

"What does Paul have to do with you Fred?" The detective inquired.

"I'm his right hand man. Nothing happens unless I know about it and I'm there," he said smugly.

"Kid, you might work for him but you're not his right hand man. Come on now, who you trying to fool?" The detective said pacing back and forth.

"I've been a witness to two murders, both high profile, and I can get you the information on another murder about to happen in the next forty eight hours," he said with confidence.

"What high profile murders are you talking about?" The one of the detectives asked now curious.

"The judge and the old D.A.," he said.

The detectives' eyes opened wide as they looked back at each other. There was something there that they could work with, but at what price?

"Let me guess, you want a get out of jail free card," the detective said.

"Just lose the video and let me walk and I'll take you right to his bed. I'll give you everything," he said.

"Tell me something, why wouldn't Paul just kill you today, because you're bringing a lot of attention to him by you being charged with first degree murder?" The detective asked.

"Paul don't know about this. I called you because my girl told me she talked to you. You didn't get the chance to put my name out on the streets nor on the news. I'm still incognito right now, and I'll stay that way if you're willing to deal," he spoke cocky because he felt he had them eating out of his hands.

"The funny thing is, we still don't know if you're lying or not. You haven't told us anything significant," the detective pointed out.

"Ok, here's something to wet your palate. The judge was shot in the right leg but his throat was cut ear to ear and hung upside down to bleed like a pig. That's how Paul felt about him," he said licking his lips.

That was a piece of information that no one could have known except those that were there. The detectives both pulled up chairs as they both were now interested in what Fred had to say.

"Alright Fred, you got our attention, what else?" The other detective asked.

"Hold up, we haven't made a deal yet," he said, sitting back.

"Let's say we had a fire and the DVD got burned. What's there to make you keep your word?" He asked the kid.

"Paul likes to video all of his murders, call it a power trip but he likes to show it to the boys who weren't there. It makes them fear him. It makes them think he'll do anything to them if they betray him. Then after he makes them watch it, he burns it," he explained.

"Ok so there's no hard proof. Again, why would we make a deal with you?" The detective asked.

"I went to school and majored in film and production management. I had to learn how to use the most high tech cameras. I dropped out simply because of money, that's how I hooked up with Paul. I figured once I got the money, I would go back and finish," he explained.

"Wow, thanks for the background history and sob story but what does that have to do with the price of tea in China?" Asked the now agitated detective.

"If you'd stop interrupting maybe you'd find out," he said staring at the detective. He gave him the go ahead to finish.

"Like I was saying, I'm good with all types of cameras. I have a camera that I stole from this big time movie producer, don't ask me how but I did it. It actually films on DVD but saves a copy on the hard drive automatically so should anything happen to the DVD, you have a backup," the kid said smiling.

The light went off as both detectives smiled. Neither spoke, they wanted to hear more.

"So everything that I've filmed, I still have. The hard drive is built into a case that's made of the same material as the black boxes on planes, so should anything ever happen to the camera, the hard drive is still good. No one knows this but me, so the info that I just gave you should buy all the tea in China," he said smiling.

The detective rubbed the scruff growing on his face. He wanted more proof if he was going to make a deal.

"I want to see something, let me see one video. Give me something undisputable that would make my DVD player catch on fire and burn the ONLY evidence we have against you," the detective said staring at Fred.

"Alright, I'll give you one. That bag that you took from me when I got here, it had that camera in it," he said as he smiled at the haste the detectives made to get the camera out of the bag to view the evidence. When they got the camera out, they saw it was locked with an encrypted code. They didn't have time to unlock it so they brought it back in the interrogation room for Fred to unlock it.

"Look, don't play games. It's your life that's on the line here," the detective warned.

Fred unlocked the camera and pulled up one of the videos and allowed both detectives to watch a senseless and heinous crime being committed. They were both disgusted and ecstatic at the same time. Once the video was finished, they both left the room for a period of time then came back. Apparently Paul was more important.

"Dang it, seems like my machine caught on fire and burned up the only piece of evidence we had against you, oh but look," he said as he pulled out another DVD from behind his back like it was magic, "I think this is a copy," he said as he sat down across from Fred.

"Ok so what's the new deal?" Fred asked.

"I want in on this murder that's going to happen in forty eight hours. I want a copy of that murder that you have on your camera that one and every other one you have on there," he said pointing at the camera.

"I want immunity and I won't wear a wire. We get checked too often. And I want a new life somewhere out of the country. I don't plan on coming back," Fred said as he thought of the possible repercussions.

"You that scared of this kid? You put me in there and I'm putting him on death row," the detective said trying to assure the young man.

"You put him on death row and he still has an arm on the streets. I don't want that arm touching me" he said full of fear.

"What about your kids?" the other detective asked.

"What about them? They gotta learn how to survive just like I did," he said looking down. Both detectives looked at the young man in disgust. They discussed it further but the F.B.I. wanted Paul James so badly that they were willing to go along with the deal Fred was making.

Fred left the F.B.I. building at one and headed to where Paul and the rest of the crew were. He pulled up to the two-story house at one thirty five on the dot. Fred didn't know that news of his time spent with the feds was already common knowledge.

Paul watched his friend come in and sit down on the couch across from him. He watched him closely, what was he doing with the feds?

"Where you been at? I been calling you all day," Paul said as he stared at Fred.

Fred knew better than to lie, he knew Paul had to have known his whereabouts by his question. He never asked where you've been if he wasn't suspicious of your activity. He knew this game better than anyone and he would play it like chess.

"I been in the dragon's lair, bruh" he said smiling.

"Where?" Paul asked, looking confused.

"With the feds man. Had me down there questioning me about the dude that tried to holla at my girl," he said.

"What about him?" asked Paul.

"He's dead. Got shot once in the head," he told him.

"You did it?" Paul smiled now.

"Not this time, doesn't mean I wasn't going to though. Dude got what he deserved," he said.

"Take your clothes off" Paul said suddenly.

Fred was confused. He looked around to see six guys starting to surround him.

"Man I'm your right hand, why would you think I'm wearing a wire? All that we been through and you think I'm going to betray you now?" He asked, now standing.

"If you don't take them off, they'll gladly help you," he said pointing to the other guys in the room.

"Why would I tell you I've been with the feds then wear a wire over here? Paul, everybody ain't ya enemy man," he said frowning angrily.

"If you have nothing to worry about then just strip. Freddie, no one is immune, stop taking it so personal!" Paul said sarcastically.

Fred did as he was told, he stripped till he was naked and Paul was satisfied.

"Put your clothes back on Freddie. You could never be too careful, not even with your own hands," he said quietly as he got up and left the room. All the other guys laughed at him and cracked jokes, but Fred remained serious. He wanted Paul's demise even more than the feds. Forty-eight hours and it would all be over he thought to himself as he got dressed. Forty-eight.

# CHAPTER 12

*Ephesians 4:22-24* *That ye put off concerning the former conversation the old man, which is corrupt according to the deceitful lusts; (23) And be renewed in the spirit of your mind; (24) And that ye put on the new man, which after God is created in righteousness and true holiness.*

When Sondra got saved. She changed a lot of things in her life. She had big hopes, dreams and aspirations to consider. She only wanted people who were positive and uplifting around her. If you didn't have any goals or plans in life, or if you weren't aspiring to do anything, she simply couldn't be bothered with you. She surrounded herself with people who either have attained or is in the process of attaining their goals. She made sure that if you were in the past, you stayed in the past. She changed her phone numbers, got a new and better job, and stopped hanging out in places that she knew wasn't the right atmosphere for her. She completely changed her mind about the life she once lived to live the life she deserves to live.

Timothy has been the best man she's ever dated. He doesn't just talk the talk, but walks it as well. He doesn't bring up sex or touches her inappropriately. He loves spending time with her on the beach, or at parks. There they have all the time to walk and hold hands while talking about God and life in general. She knows all about his past but is only focused on his future just like he is of hers. They push each other and she's never had anyone that cares about her do that. Timothy made her very happy but what she really had was Joy. She knew she had haters, but she wasn't about to let them ruin this good thing so she kept her business to herself and kept her eyes on God. She just didn't know, watch the ones that are the closest to you and not those that are the farthest.

The phone rings and Sondra stares at the caller id. "Who could this be?" she wonders to herself before answering.

"Hello?" She answered.

"Hey Sondra, how are you?" The voice said on the other end.

"Who is this?" She asked.

"Dang you forgot my voice already?" The male voice asked laughing.

"Michael?!" She said as her voice rose slightly.

"The one and the only," he answered.

"How did you get my number?" She said, now annoyed.

"I saw your mom and she gave it to me, do you mind?" He asked.

"Yes actually I do mind. NO ONE is supposed to give my number to anyone without first getting my approval," she said matter of factly.

"It's like that now? I mean, we got history. We used to be together for years, maybe that's why she thought she could give it to me," he said defensively.

"I understand that, but the past is why I do the things I do now," she said in answer to his rebuttal.

"Ouch, I guess that means me," he said acting like he was hurt by her comment.

"You're included but you're not the only one. So did you call just to hear my voice or is there a reason?" She asked, not interested in the small talk at all.

"Well I called because I heard about your dad and I wanted you to know I'm sorry for your loss," he said solemnly.

"Thank you Michael, I appreciate that," she said rolling her eyes.

"So is tonight a good night for dinner?" He asked.

"Every night is a good night for dinner but if you mean with you then the answer is no," she said as she flopped down on the couch not believing the nerve of her ex.

"Why not? What else you doing? Oh yea, your mom told me you was so into the church now or could it be the crack head you been stringing along?" He asked smugly.

Sondra couldn't believe what she was hearing, how did her mother know about Tim? She was too nosey but she's had it and was about to let him and her mother know...enough is enough!

"Excuse me? I don't know who told you or my mother to mind my dern business, but both of y'all can step the heck up out of my life. How dare you call me asking me

168

questions about my business? Do me a favor Mike and get some business of your own," she said angrily.

"Whoa whoa whoa, slow your roll Sondra. Dang, I didn't mean to upset you. You know your mom is only trying to look out for you. I apologize for offending you; let's just move past this. So where you working at now, I went by your old job to drop off some flowers when I heard about your dad and they said you resigned. They wouldn't tell me where you went from there," he said trying his hardest to change the subject.

"Mike, maybe I'm not making myself clear enough for you. I meant what I said; mind your business when it comes to me. You don't need to know where I work, you don't need to take me to dinner, and you don't need to call me anymore. Thank you for your condolences, but call it a day and go kick rocks!" She said as she hung up.

Sondra was livid by now. She couldn't believe her mom would do something like this when she specifically told her not to give her number to Michael. She had to call her; she needed closure.

"Hey sugar," the chirpy voice answered.

"No this ain't sugar, matter of fact, I have no idea who that is. Ma, why would you give Michael my number when I told you specifically not to?" Sondra asked.

"Well I'm having a great day, how about you?" Her mother answered sarcastically.

"I'm so not interested in your jokes. Could you please just answer my question?" Sondra was getting impatient now.

"Sondra, Michael has changed. He's matured into this fine man AND he's even admitted he's messed up with you. He

169

wants to get it right Sondra, give the man a chance," she pleaded with her.

"I don't care if he turned into the Pope himself, you are supposed to call me first," she said raising her voice.

"I don't feel like I need to get permission from you for anything. You're not the boss of me," she stated boldly.

"What the ham and cheese does that have to do with anything? I'm not saying I'm the boss of anybody but when it comes to me and what belongs to me, you do have to get my permission. And if you don't feel like you should then that can be easily taken care of as well," Sondra said rolling her neck like her mom could see her.

"Oh so you're going to change it again and not tell me? Ha! Do it then," she dared.

"Consider it done," Sondra had enough.

"So you're going to keep running from your past?" Her mother asked.

"I don't expect you to understand me when I say I'm focused and don't need any distractions. That's what happens when you've changed for the best and is going forward," she answered as respectfully as she could.

"Well excuse me miss high and mighty. You just like your daddy, that's why I left his behind," her mother said sharply.

"And he got along quite well without you and so will I," Sondra answered, knowing it was going to make her mother angry.

"You know what Sondra, I'm not going to feed into that at all, because you think you something cause he left you with a little bit of money and some other stuff. Don't think you better than me or got more than me, cause if you did then you wouldn't be working now," she said in frustration.

"What? Where did that come from? Oh you trying to find out exactly how much he did leave me. Well that's on a need to know basis and you don't need to know. But I will tell you this, I don't HAVE to work if I don't WANT to work," Sondra said as she sat back down on her couch. She was telling the truth; her father left her with everything he owned and all the money in the bank (and out). He had a ton of investments that were doing well so she didn't have to do anything. Sondra basically was living off of the interest the money was making that was in the bank.

"I don't know why you think it's ok to disrespect me but anyway. I need your help moving my place around because I'm hosting a little get together here tonight. Are you too angry with me to help me with that?"

"Fine, what time?" Sondra asked reluctantly. She didn't want to help but was going to just because she was her mother.

"Be here in an hour, don't be late. I really need you to be time conscious today," she said.

"I'll be there mother," she said as she hung up. Sondra went upstairs and took a shower and got ready. She put on some jeans, an old t-shirt and her sneakers.

She still wasn't in a pleasant mood though because the one person she wanted to speak to wasn't answering her calls. She was beginning to think she might have said something he didn't like, or did something he didn't like. The more she thought about it was the more she knew she was innocent. So why wasn't Timothy answering her or calling her back. She began to worry because this just wasn't like him. He always answered her calls or at least called back, why was today so different?

Sondra got to her mother's house with time to spare. She refused to use the key so she rang the doorbell instead, something she knew her mother hated.

"Why don't you just use your key like any other normal daughter would?" Her mother asked as she slung the door open.

"Because I don't want to," Sondra answered as she walked in and slipped out of her sneakers. No shoes, was her mother's policy inside her house, unless you were a first time visitor.

"I'm so glad you're here. I was hoping you'd dress better but oh well, this'll have to do," she said in a sing song voice.

"Have to do for what? I'm not staying for your party; you can get that thought out of your m..." Sondra said as she stopped short of what she was saying. Standing in her mother's living room was none other than Michael, set up from the start.

"Mom, why is Michael in your living room?" she asked frowning.

"Now don't be mad but I thought maybe if you saw him then you would change your mind about him," she said smiling widely to throw in some humor.

"Oh so you think this is a game, you think it's alright for you to intervene in my life?" Sondra's temper was rising fast.

"Somebody needs to intervene with you dating a crack addict," her mother said viciously.

"He's an ex addict and he's none of your business. That's why you by yourself now, nobody want to be fooled up with you. You always in some mess cause you always in somebody's business. How dare you?" Sondra was about to say something when her phone began vibrating. She forgot she was still holding it. When she looked at the caller id, it was Timothy. She would pause for him. She just looked at her mother then at Michael and walked out to answer her phone.

"Did I do something to you that I don't know about?" she asked immediately.

"No baby, you didn't do anything wrong. I just been dealing with a lot today," he said shaking his head.

"What's going on? They still messing with you about your license?" she was concerned.

"Naw, actually I got them today. My older brother Jason was found shot to death off of Pearl Street this morning," he broke the news to her.

"Oh my God Timothy, I'm so sorry. Where are you?" she asked.

"I'm at home," he answered.

"Can I come over? Actually I'm coming over, just give me directions," she said, not giving him a choice in the matter.

"Sondra, that's so rude of you to leave your guest to take a phone call," her mother yelled from behind her.

"Where are you?" he asked when he heard the yelling.

"My mom's house, but I'm leaving now. When I get in the car I'm going to call you back for directions," she said as she hung up on him.

"Mom, this is totally trifling of you. I'm not staying, I have somewhere more important to be right now," she said as she began to walk away.

"I planned this for you. This boy is the best for you, not that crack head you're dating now. Stop being all stuck up and come back in here. Michael already said he would take you back," her mother yelled, making a scene for her neighbors.

"This is what you do, entertain. Well you have an audience, go entertain him," with that Sondra jumped in her car and called Timothy back. He guided her to his house while staying on the phone with her the entire time. When she got there, he was standing outside to greet her.

Sondra jumped out of her car and right into Tim's arms. He held her so tight that he thought he was squeezing the breath out of her so he lightened his grip but hers never slipped. He smiled at how hard she was holding onto him, like she was the one holding him up. She was a good half a foot shorter than he was so he just bent down and kissed her on her forehead. She looked up at him with teary eyes, she didn't know.

"Don't you let not one tear drop Shawty. It ain't that type of party. I mean my mom is hurting but I'm ok, I just been here all day with her that's all." He said looking down at her.

"But Tim, that was your brother," she said not understanding his statement at all.

"Jason was a little different," he said as they walked over and sat on the hood of her car, "he was my father's son by another woman. The woman died and left Jason in my

174

dad's custody. So of course, my mom being who she is, raised him as one of her own. He was always so distant though. Once he was old enough to leave, he left and he would come around every six months or so but that's it. We didn't know anything about him. He was cool, he was funny as all out doors but that's all we could tell you about him. So when he passed away, it was almost like wow, who? Oh MY brother Jason? Oh," he said, explaining his attitude to her.

"So he wasn't close to anybody? At all? Not even a little?" she asked curiously.

"Nope! When his mom died and he got in our household, my dad died the year after. He stayed under our roof for five years cause he was thirteen when he got here. Like I said, he was cool and funny but that's all we know about Jason," Tim said as he shook his head.

"So how's your mom taking it?" she asked.

"She's hurt cause she loved Jason, no matter that he didn't let her in. She still loved him like one of her own. She's been crying all day, especially after I took her to identify the body. Then she had to make plans for his funeral and burial. We didn't even know he had a kid, three years old. His baby mama came around here to see us. Apparently he knew something was going to happen because he was prepared. She brought all the information and even brought his little girl for us to see. She looks just like him, that's scary." He said laughing.

"Dang why you say that? Was he ugly or something?" she asked trying to understand.

"Naw, none of us are ugly you know. We just all look like our dad except the girls. To see this little girl that looks just like my brother that looks just like my dad is scary," he said as he smiled at her.

"Ok now I understand," she said laughing too. "If you don't mind, I would like to give your mom my condolences," she said as she grabbed his hand.

"Of course you can, but let me warn you now, Justine and Kevin is in there." He said with a serious look on his face.

"Oh boy, I get to finally meet the hell raisers themselves?" she asked jokingly.

"Naw, you get to meet the devil and her right hand man," he said as he laughed. Sondra laughed too, she was so happy to be with Timothy, even under the circumstances. She was a little nervous because she did not know what to expect coming from his siblings. His mother, she absolutely adored, but maybe Timothy exaggerated a little...she would soon find out.

As soon as they walked through the door, Justine let them have it.

"Oh well would you look at this, the crack head brings home one of his crack hoes," she said looking at Sondra up and down. Sondra was not expecting that, after all this was a time of mourning.

"Justine, I knew it was too good to last. Take your disrespectful tail out my house now. Your father must've dropped you when you was a baby cause there's no reason to be the way you are. Why are you so nasty? Well since you want to judge, the bible says you're going to be judged. You sit here and judge this boy cause of his addiction but he had the guts to fight it. What have you done?" Andrea asked watching Justine carefully.

"I've done nothing wrong," Justine answered in her almighty way.

"Yes you have, you've had two abortions. You cheated on your husband four times and one of those times was with the pastor at your old church. Pick your lip up baby. When you do wrong to people, they enjoy spreading your business. You slept with one of your husband's lodge brothers and you slept with some young guy that couldn't keep his mouth shut. So you see Missy, you ain't no saint! You've done plenty wrong. Yeah he was a drug addict, but you STILL a hoe!" Andrea finished off with a laugh as Justine gathered her stuff and ran out the door.

When she left, the house got silent as everybody looked around to see what the other person was going to do or say. Kevin felt awkward and left shortly after acting like he was taking an important phone call. Once he left, everyone burst out in laughter. No one could believe Andrea said what she did but all was happy Justine was put on Front Street. Now that that was out the way, Andrea was able to pay attention to Sondra.

"Hey baby, come give me a hug," she said as she held out her hands to Sondra.

"I'm sorry about your son Mrs. Washington," Sondra whispered in her ears as the two women hugged.

"Oh baby, nothing to be sorry about. I love Jason and my heart breaks for his family but we didn't know him. He would never let himself go around us. His poor baby mama, she's so distraught. She said she got a call from him right before he was killed. She said in the four years they been together, this was the first time he told her he loved her. She heard the gun go off. It's really a shame. I cry hard for

177

him because he didn't have anybody Sondra, not since his mom died." Andrea said wiping more tears from her eyes.

"What's surprising is that the police said he was one of the highest ranking drug dealers in the southeast. He had a meet up today with a rival and they killed him. What's funny is they said they knew something was going to happen but they couldn't move until it did. So my brother had to die in order to catch the other guy. Then they said they found like thirty kilos of cocaine in his trunk alone, raw and uncut straight from Columbia. This thing was serious," Tim explained to Sondra.

"So they got the guy who killed your brother?" she asked taking a seat next to Andrea.

"Yea, they got him but the informant that was working for the feds was working for this dude too and he got killed. So I don't know what's going to happen now," he said as he too took a seat next to his mother.

"Holy cow, I saw something about a big drug bust, happened today on the east side. It flashed across the news but I didn't pay it any attention. Maybe it's because of his lifestyle that he stayed so distant," she said offering some kind of explanation for why Jason did them the way he did.

"Baby, in all honesty I just think Jason just never got over his mother's death," Andrea said shaking her head.

"But Ma, Sondra might have a point. You know drug dealers will come after your family in a heartbeat. I agree he's never got over her death, but I think he stayed away from us because of what he was doing." Timothy said as he played with Sondra's feet under the table.

"I don't know Timothy; my only concern now is for that child. She looks so much like him," she said as she sighed heavily.

"So was it a rival gang or just some other drug dealer?" Sondra asked Timothy.

"We don't know. The only thing we know is that it was another drug king just looking to take over more territory. They haven't released any names as of yet," he answered.

"Oh Timothy, how could I forget son? I have some great news for you," Andrea said reaching across the table grabbing his hands.

"Ok Ma wassup? I need some right about now," Timothy said as he looked at his mother then at the woman he knew he was falling in love with.

"Simone is coming home, she'll be here tomorrow. She's on a plane right now from Germany," she told him. Timothy smiled ear to ear. Simone was his favorite sister in the whole world. She had his back even when he was in the streets. She had to take care of her business, which had her flying all over Europe. But she was headed home now and things were going to start getting real interesting.

Timothy got up from the table and bear hugged his mother and they both laughed in joy. The odds would finally be even.

Sondra didn't leave till almost three in the morning to go home. Even though today went from being dramatic to being sad to being exhilarating, she wasn't tired. Timothy kissed her before she got in her car and that's all she could think of on the way home. Her body was begging her to go back but her heart told her to wait, it would be worth it. She listened to her heart tonight, it better be right.

179

*3 **John** 1:2 Beloved, I wish above all things that thou mayest prosper and be in health, even as thy soul prospereth.*

Karen cooked a roast, some cabbage, macaroni and cheese, then changed it up a little and made a to-die-for pumpkin pie. She took three plates up to the hospital for her two favorite men but she took the whole pie just in case. They can both eat like ravenous beasts. Karen got to the hospital at one fifteen and walked right into Shawn's room only to find a cute little visitor.

"Oh hello there," she said to the young lady. "Didn't know you had a guest, I would've knocked first, then walked in," she said smiling as she put the food in front of Shawn.

"Thanks Ma, but uh how's Sam? You going to visit him right?" he said, as he signaled her with his one good eye to get out.

"Let me get this right, I slave over the stove for hours trying to make sure you have good food and I get kicked out AND I don't even get an introduction. I thought I deserved a little better treatment than that. Wait I know, gimmie my food back," she joked as she playfully reached for the plate of food that was set up right in front of Shawn.

"Waaaaait a minute lady; Taylor this beautiful lady to my right is my mother, Mother meet Taylor," he tried to make the introduction as short and sweet as possible.

"Why do you look so familiar to me Taylor?" Karen said staring at the young lady.

"My dad and Officer Preston work together and we go to the same church so that's probably where you saw me at. That's where I remember you from," Taylor said smiling at Karen.

"Ok so I get how we know each other, but how do you two know each other? Because he don't come to church," Karen inquired of Taylor.

"I usually volunteer at the hospital on Thursdays for their teen nurse movement and my mom is his day nurse and that's how I met him," she said pointing at Shawn.

"Mom, you're eating with Sam right? Cause I'm sure he's starving right about now," he said practically begging her to leave.

"Ok Shawn, I'm leaving but I'm coming back. Love you, give me a kiss," she said as she bent close to him for her kiss.

"Aww Ma, come on with the mushy stuff," he said turning away his face.

"Ok let's make this simple, you don't kiss me, I will embarrass you" she said with a look on his face that he understood that she would do as she said. Needless to say he kissed her. Karen left the two lovebirds alone and made her way down the hall to Sam's room. She's been here every day since that night and she loves every minute they spend together. As she turned the corner, it was to see a beautiful young woman standing there. She had the deepest brown eyes and beautiful auburn hair she's ever seen. She was not model thin, but you could tell she was in great shape. That smile, she knew this was the daughter he always spoke of.

"Hey Karen, come on in. I would like you to meet my daughter Esther, Baby Girl, this is Karen," he said as he watched the two women meet for the first time.

"Wow, you're absolutely gorgeous. Your father said you look like your mom so I know she had to be stunning." She said as she embraced the young lady.

"Gee thank you, that's the sweetest thing anyone has ever said to me, especially just meeting me," Esther said as she smiled to her daddy. "Well, I have go now. I have to pick my little one up, go home and cook. See you later daddy, and it was nice meeting you Karen. We'll have to do lunch or something," she said as she kissed her father and left.

Sam motioned for Karen to sit down by him as she prepared his plate of food in front of him. He looked at the food then looked at her, said his grace and dove in like an Olympic diver.

"I think she actually likes you" he said between chews.

"Sam your daughter is gorgeous. How many guys did you have to shoot over her?" she asked watching the corners of his lips go up in a smile.

"Many, but I can't tell you who and where I've hidden the bodies," he said jokingly.

"How was physical therapy today?"

"One word, brutal."

"Please tell me you didn't kick the therapist again," she said as she laughed as she remembered the incident.

"I bet they stopped when I said stop this time," he said as he swallowed some cabbage.

"Did they tell you a release date yet?" she asked.

"Yea, the second" he said as he tipped the plate to drink the juice in the plate.  Karen sat there and watched him laughing.

"Hey that's the day after Shawn gets out," she blurted out.

"Great so you think you can come pick me up too?" he asked as he started looking for something else to devour.

"Sam, where did you put all that food that just I fixed for you? You know that's not normal don't you," she said as he laughed and patted his stomach.  "And yes I can come get you, Shawn ain't going nowhere," she added.

"You mean you cooked all this food and didn't make any desert? I find that hard to believe.  What about that sweet potato pie, did you make some more of that?" he asked greedily.

"Sam I came to eat with you and you swallowed yours and I haven't even touched mine.  Now you want to ask me for some pies.  No I didn't make sweet potato, I made pumpkin instead and before you say anything taste it first," she said as she cut him a piece of the pie and gave it to him.

"Only cause it's you, but I don't normally eat pumpkin," he said as he put half the slice in his mouth gave her a funny look then put the rest in his mouth.  "Oh please baby, just give me the rest of the pie.  I don't know what you put in these pies, but lawd have mercy they're so good." He was begging her for another slice.

Karen ended up giving Sam the rest of the pie in which he commenced to smash.  Thank God she never told Shawn about the pie.  They sat there for hours just talking and talking, something Sam loved to do.  He told old police stories about the criminals he met in the streets and funny stories about his kids. He wanted her to know everything there was to know about him; the good, the bad and the ugly. Karen listened; she enjoyed hearing him speak. He made the funniest faces and he took you into the story to where you felt like you were right beside him when whatever he spoke about was happening.

Karen told him of some of her past, especially of her ex husband and how he became ex. Sam listened to all the hurt and pain Karen went through with one man and knew she still needed healing. She was such a humble and caring woman, she reminded him of his wife in that aspect. The two women were very different and that's what he liked about her, she wasn't trying to fill his dead wife's shoes.

Sam watched her and decided to go for it. When it was time for her to leave and she leaned over to hug him, he kissed her instead. She kissed him back. Karen was all smiles and blushes when she left his room without a word. It seemed like she floated back to Shawn's room because her body and lips were still with Sam. She opened Shawn's door only to find him asleep so she kissed him and left.

Sam laid there in another world, she had the softest lips. He wasn't used to just kissing people but he couldn't fight the urge any longer with her. All he could do is smile and dream, dream of candy kisses from the sweetest woman.

# CHAPTER 13

*2 Corinthians 5:17* *Therefore if any man be in Christ, he is a new creature: old things are passed away; behold, all things are become new.*

Sondra was preparing to go back to Tim's house when the phone rings. She answers without looking at the caller id, something she just never does. She assumed it would be Tim; somehow the voice just doesn't sound the same.

"Hey sexy," she said as she answered the phone.

"Hey yourself beautiful," Mike said at the salutation.

"Oh my god, are you serious? Michael what do you want?" she asked instantly frustrated.

"Dang, how do you go from hey sexy to what do you want?" Michael asked sensing her frustration.

"Because I can't believe you're calling me after I politely asked you not to," she said putting her bag down on the counter.

"I'm the persistent type," he responded.

"Can you be persistent with somebody who actually wants you and not somebody who doesn't?" she struck a blow.

"Oh so you don't want me now? You'd rather choose a crack head over me? Was I that bad to you Sondra?" he asked as his anger was kindled.

"Oh em gee Mike, so what he's an ex addict. That's his past and you're mine, we're moving forward together. And why do you care about who I'm dating all of a sudden?"

"What do you mean why do I care? I'm trying to make you my wife and I got this crack head standing in my way, that's why I care" he said as he began pacing.

"Your wife? Ha! You haven't been in my life in over two years then you pop up out of nowhere and think I'm going to marry you like that? Please tell me how that works. Oh so cause you lifted some weights, brush your hair now and bought a few suits you think I should fall prostrate before your awesome masculinity and we ride off into the sunset together?" she asked completely frustrated now.

"I just don't understand you; even your mother says I'm a good catch. If she can see that, why can't you?" he asked as he sat back down.

"Yea you're a catch, you're just not what I'm looking for that's why I threw you back," she said as she grabbed her purse and headed out. She wasn't about to let him postpone her plans anymore.

"So you are holding the past against me," he said as he jumped to his feet like he had an epiphany.

"No Michael, I'm not holding the past against you, I'm just not interested in having a future with you. It's time you moved on because I have already," she said as she started up her car and began heading to Tim's house.

"Moved on with what? I can't believe that you would choose this guy over me. I'm dumbfounded by your decision to walk away from everything I'm offering you," he said like he was really hurt.

"Mike, I told God I wasn't going back. That included you, so take everything you're offering and give it to someone else. As far as I'm concerned, we're not going to have another conversation," she said making it clear this was their last.

"Sondra, I'm the best shot you got to a dream. You better jump on me before somebody else does and you end up looking stupid in the face," he said in a warning tone.

"You know what Mike, that's a chance I'm willing to take. You have a nice life and I wish nothing but the best for you, but you're not the best for me," she said making sure he knew their conversation was nearing its end.

"Yea, you're beneath me anyway if you think a crack head is best for you," he said arrogantly.

With that Sondra hung up. She called her phone service right away and had her number changed again to another non-published number. This time, she learned her lesson. Her mother was not going to get her number.

Timothy paced the floor several times as his mother watched. She smiled knowing how nervous he was, she just didn't understand. He was only asking her to go to the funeral with him. When the doorbell rang, he nearly jumped out of his skin he was so enthralled in his thoughts. As he opened the door for her, he practically threw up on her.

"Will you come to the funeral with me?" he blurted out.

"Well hey baby and I only naturally assumed that since we're a couple that I would be going with you." She said as she kissed him lightly on his lips and smiled.

Timothy breathed again and moved out of her way so she could enter the house. He couldn't imagine what a mess he would be like asking her to marry him if he was this nervous about a funeral. He was thinking about marriage, he even asked Pastor if it was too soon to be thinking about marriage, if they've only been dating for a few months. His Pastor made him think, "How long does it take to know you really love someone and who set those guidelines?" Timothy loved Sondra and he couldn't hide it from anyone, although he thought he was. She loved him as well and thought the same. Andrea smiled as she watched the two of them interact with each other, the stares, the smiles, the light touches and blushes. They were a beautiful couple and she knew they loved each other. This was one relationship she approved of whole-heartedly.

The two of them took Andrea on last minute errands and finally to the funeral home to add last minute touches and to view the body before the actual viewing that was being held that night. Andrea cried as she walked up to the body of Jason Washington, dead at thirty-two. He was so handsome lying there in an all black silk suit. He had it all planned, even down to the type of shirt he wanted to be buried in. Timothy viewed the body of his brother, now an empty shell. He looked and seen the hole in the side of his head behind his ear. The parlor did a good job trying to cover the bullet hole but you could still tell it was there.

"Goodbye son, there's so much I wanted to share with you but you wouldn't let me. The one thing I can say is you knew I loved you. I told you every chance I got," she whispered to him as she patted his chest and walked away drying her eyes.

"You alright Ma?" Timothy asked concerned.

"I needed to see him because now I can let him go. I didn't want to let him go in front of everybody because then I would be too emotional. Thank you both for bringing me," she said as she just stood there looking to heaven in prayer.

"You know why I raised him Timothy?" she turned to her son to see his face.

"No Ma," he answered looking back at her.

"Because I had the ability to. Nothing deep, no spiritual moment, an angel didn't descend from Heaven and light up my room and told me to do it. I didn't hear the voice of God, heck; I didn't even know God then. I just had the ability to help. When Bruce asked me could Jason come live with us, I didn't hesitate; I just made room for him. That child needed a home and a family, and I gave it to him. He grew up and made his own decisions and lived his own life. And now he's dead." The tears started to run down her face. "I'm sorry I had a moment there. I guess I just wanted to vent a little bit," she said as she stepped closer to Timothy.

Timothy wrapped his arms around his mother; she hugged him back and cried into his chest. Sondra rubbed her back in an attempt to comfort her as she too had tears in her eyes.

"It's alright Ma, vent as much as you want. I have the ability to take it" he said softly as he bent down and kissed her on her tear stained cheeks.

**Psalms 119:93** *I will never forget thy precepts: for with them thou hast quickened me.*

It was Monday, the first of October and time for Shawn to go home. It's been two months, thirteen days and eleven hours. Karen was there doing all the necessary and unnecessary paperwork for the release of her son. She knows she'll be right back up here again tomorrow to get Sam but today she was going to just focus on Shawn. She didn't really know how, with Sam consuming her thoughts the way he has been with his kisses and smiles. Karen got all the last minute instructions for Shawn's home care then turned around to see the happiest young man on the planet.

"Ma I actually get to sleep in my own bed tonight," he said as he swung his legs out the bed while the nurses helped him to his custom made wheel chair.

"I'm so glad you're coming home baby boy. Your dad said he will come to the house and sit with you a few days out the week until you can handle being alone again," she said as she wheeled him down the hallway. Shawn waved good bye to all of the nurses and friends he made in the almost two and a half months he's been there as they brought him balloons and cards and gave him tons of kisses. He almost felt like he was in a fantasy.

"Ma, you think Taylor could come to the house and see me sometimes?" he asked as she pulled him into the elevator.

"As long as I'm home and the both of you are downstairs in the living room," she said watching his reflecting in the elevator doors.

"I can handle that. So when does Sam come home?" he asked knowing it had to be soon.

"He's going home tomorrow. I asked your dad to come sit with you tomorrow because I'm coming to pick him up and take him home and make sure everything is good there."

"So you going to be gone all day?"

"Pretty much, why you ask that?" she asked as the elevator doors opened up on their floor.

"Oh I just thought you were going to drop him off and come back home," he said as he adjusted himself in the seat.

"He doesn't have anyone to take care of him like you do, so I'm going to help him out a little that's all," she explained as she pulled him next to her truck so he can shift himself into it.

"So when am I going to meet this dude? After all, this is the cop that saved my life. I would like to thank him personally," he said as she closed the door to get in the driver side.

"I'll ask him to come by then," she said as they drove home. This was the first time since that fateful night that Shawn was able to see outside. He was glad to have scenery to watch. He sat quiet as he seen the neighborhoods go by in a blur. He saw some people he knew but most he didn't, but he missed everything he was viewing. He even missed the smell of the retention ponds and the Jamaican bakery on the corner. Soon he was home; he looked up to heaven and knew somebody up there was looking out for him down here.

"Travis, let me ask you a question," Christina said as she interrupted her husband watching CNN.

"Wassup babe?" he asked as muted the television.

"You pray for Tyrone right? She asked sitting down next to Travis.

"Yea, why you ask me that?" he said looking confused.

"Guess I'm just worried about all the souls that he's affecting. I mean he's going to all these places and men from all over the world come to hear the word of God. I'm worried that he's spitting venom on them and their dying slowly without a clue," she said looking worried.

"Babe, God takes venom and makes anti venom. The toxicity is made ineffective so that healing can take place. The one thing I know is that God uses this man; he is a willing vessel. Everything that God does through him is authentic. Now the life he lives is not of God but it doesn't affect what God is doing. The one thing I know about God, Baby, is that if you're serving HIM and you're not living right, HE's going to reveal you to others. Either we get it straight or HE's going to straighten it," he said to her as she leaned into him on the couch.

"I understand what you're saying but these men have their souls wide open, and anything can flow into them," she stated.

"I don't agree with that," he replied as he watched her reaction.

"You don't? Then what do you think?" She is sitting up now.

"When a person comes expecting a move of God, that's what they get. But when a person comes expecting a move of man, they get everything else. They get whatever demons and spirits are floating around waiting for willing vessels, preying on the ones that come to see Tyrone Baxter. The spirit of God is in that place waiting for those that come to see him," he explained to her as he too sat up.

"Ok that makes sense. I guess my fear comes into play because I know when he is revealed; a whole lot of men is going to need help dealing with this, especially those in ministry. They'll wonder why they didn't catch it sooner," she said as she watched Travis get up from his seat.

"You know I won't feel sorry for the men in ministry. If they paid more attention to the spirit than to the man, then they would know what kind of man they're dealing with. God is not just going to reveal Tyrone; he's going to reveal them in their ignorance," he said being slightly agitated.

"I didn't mean to upset you Baby," she said trying to calm him down. Travis walked back over to the couch and flopped back down.

"I'm not upset Babe; it's just that it's one thing to say that these people didn't know better. But to say these men, who have been pastoring for years and ministering to people who have the same spirit, don't know better is an insult and a blow to the Church as a whole. How can they preach, don't pay attention to man if that's all they pay attention to? They mock God, but HE will not be mocked," he said shaking his head in disgust. Travis and Christine sat there and continued to watch CNN together.

There was news of terrorists, news of murders everywhere, news of storms and power outages. Celebrity news came on and there was his smiling face. Tyrone Baxter commands sold out crowds all over the country. Travis is sickened by the man on the TV oozing all over Tyrone like he's some kind of god. The woman is gushing all sorts of compliments on how fine he is and how positive his image is for the youth today.

They comment on everything from how sharp he dresses, to how straight his teeth are, to how clean his haircut looks. They look and lavish on the outside of this man without truly knowing the truth. Travis wonders what will happen once the truth comes out. Those same commentators will turn rude and hateful. Their compliments will turn into homophobic words of hate and disdain. They exalted him now, later their going to yell hang him!

*Proverbs 18:22* *Whoso findeth a wife findeth a good thing, and obtaineth favour of the LORD.*

Sondra finally met Simone; she instantly fell in love with her.  It was almost immediate that she could tell why Timothy loved his sister so much.  She was down to earth and warm.  She loved to smile and enjoyed life to the fullest.  The most important thing was that Simone loved Sondra as well.  The funeral went on without a hitch. Justine and Kevin did come but sat quietly as Simone eyed them the whole time daring them to move an inch.  The two went their separate ways after the burial.  They all went back to Andrea's house for the re past except for Jason's baby and her mother.  They decided to go back to where she was from in Philadelphia so she can be closer to family. She promised to keep in touch as she left the funeral to go straight to the airport.

Andrea was not as sad as she thought she would be.  Maybe it was because she had a future daughter-in-law on her mind.  Timothy told her he decided to ask the question, so she gave him her wedding set Bruce gave to her.  As everyone else left the car to go in the house, he asked Sondra to stay.  Would she say yes?  He would soon find out.

"Honey why are we sitting in the car?" she asked "And why are you sweating so much?" she said wiping his head with her handkerchief.

"Sondra I really care for you, matter of fact I just outright love you," he said, barely looking at her.

"I love you too baby," she said as she smiled showing all of her teeth. She was smiling so hard; she didn't notice him fidgeting with something in his right hand.

"I'm glad to hear you say that, say um, do you think you could spend the rest of your life with me?" he asked hesitantly.

"No I don't think so, I know I could," she said confidently.

"I know the timing isn't perfect with the funeral and all but if I wait any longer I'll lose my nerve. I'm asking you to be my wife, will you marry me Sondra?" He finally got the words past the lump in his throat.

Sondra looked down at the ring and tears came gushing out of her eyes. She was beside herself with happiness. She flexed her hand so he could put it on her finger, then she reached over to kiss and whisper, "yes" on his lips. Timothy hugged her soundly. He jumped out the car and yelled to the top of his voice, "she said YESSSSSS!" His mother came to the door, hearing his loud yelling and started to celebrate as well. This day wasn't ending on the same note it began on.

Andrea laid one son to rest, as the other was about to begin a new journey. Simone had been away from Florida for ten years living in Germany. She decided it was time to move back home. There was no better timing than the present. The pastor was over at the house when all the happiness and jubilation started so he sat the both of them down and told them the importance of marriage counseling. They set up sessions to begin as soon as the next day. The easiest decision was whether or not they were going to have a wedding. Sondra wasn't so big on one since her dad died but wanted a small one and Timothy wasn't big on the idea but they both decided to have one next year as well as their honeymoon. Andrea laughed in Joy, the one they told her wasn't going to make it, is making it!

*James 2:13 For he shall have judgment without mercy, that hath shewed no mercy; and mercy rejoiceth against judgment.*

Paul stood at the rendezvous point with his boys in their position. For the first time in his life, he's nervous. Something just didn't seem right. Freddie was fidgety, like he was expecting something to go wrong, but Paul chalked that up to nerves. All he could think of was becoming King, King of the drug world. All would fear him; some would love him but most would hate him. The Mexicans and Columbians would want to work with him once they knew he took over. His plan was plain and simple, shake hands then shoot to kill. He was willing to take another bullet to be on top if that's what it took.

Freddie stood there watching and waiting. He knew who was watching but he just had a feeling in the pit of his stomach that things just weren't going to go according to plan. He didn't know what to do at this point so he tried to calm himself with thoughts of leaving the country once this was over. When his heart rate was under control, he looked over at Paul who looked rather edgy himself. He dreamed of killing him and hoped today was the day of his demise. He blamed Paul for the nightmares and for the emotionless ranting of a lunatic's mind at times. He also blamed Paul for his cousin's death, trying to earn a spot on his team. Freddie wondered at what point were they going to make their move, was there going to be a murder at all?

Jason knew the person he was meeting very well. He knew what he wanted and why, but he would humor him. He watched his opponent closely and knew his every step and move, nothing surprised him. Jason felt in his heart, this was a wrong move to make so he brought extra gun power just in case. He felt his phone vibrate and read the text from his girlfriend that said she loved him; he smiled. Today, he would tell her, she would hear him say the words she longed for. As he stepped around the corner and saw Paul, his call connected. Jason was amazed at how young Paul looked, he reminded him of his younger brother, just deadlier. As Jason shook Paul's hands, he whispered the last three words of his life to his girl, I LOVE YOU. Then everything went black.

As the bullets whizzed past Paul, everything seemed to have moved in slow motion. Everyone was falling around him but nothing was hitting him. Paul wasn't nervous at this point at all as he eyed the dead body on the ground, he knew it was done. He was now the drug kingpin of the southeastern United States. Just as reality started to speed up Paul caught glimpse of the familiar lights of police cruisers. He knew at that moment he was set up and began to run. He noticed as guys tried to come to his aide, they were being shot dead; there was a sniper somewhere. Paul knew he could not run anywhere and do anything. When he looked for Freddie, it was to find him beside Jason, dead. Paul was the only one left standing at this point as everyone else who was able to get away, ran. It seemed like every policeman and woman in Jacksonville Florida came out to arrest him, but it was only one who put the cuffs on and read him his rights.

"Paul James, you are under arrest for trafficking of a controlled substance, being in possession of a controlled substance with the intent to sell and twelve counts of murder in the first degree. You have the right to remain silent, everything you say can and will be used against you in a court of law. You have the right to an attorney. If you cannot afford one, one will be appointed to you. Do you understand your rights?" Detective Rich asked him as he placed him up against the police cruiser.

"Yea I understand," Paul said as the officers frisked him.

"Do you want to tell your side of the story Paul or are you waiving your right to speak?" he asked, knowing what Paul would do.

"Talk to my lawyer," Paul said, voice almost in a whisper.

Detective Rich got up close to Paul so only he could hear what was being said.

"How long did you think this was going to last? In one day you became a king and in the same day you were made a prisoner; no longer having an empire, no longer the head of anything. You know there are some boys waiting for you in prison. Me personally, I hope they tear you apart limb from limb," he said as they shoved him into the cruiser. Detective Rich tapped the top of the police car to let them know that it was ok to leave. Detective made sure there was no playing with this situation; he sent eight other cars to escort Paul to jail. His time finally came, and he's going to live to pay. They made sure of that.

One of the other Detectives stooped down besides Freddie's body. He apologized that his life was taken, but a price had to be paid. Detective Rich disagreed.

"Don't apologize, he got what he deserved," he said to the other detective.

"Yea I know, but we told him he would be alright," he said as he stood up.

"That was before he tried to kill Paul. We did what we had to do and in the end, it worked out for the best," Rich stated as he slapped the other detective on the back.

"Live by the gun, die by the gun" the detective said while walking away from the body.

***Song of Solomon 7:10*** *I am my beloved's, and his desire is toward me.*

The months seemed to fly by as Timothy and Sondra's wedding day came. Not very many people knew of the planned marriage because they just wanted to do something for close family and friends. The ceremony itself was to be about fifteen minutes long and then dinner at a restaurant that Simone picked out. Everyone was excited, especially Andrea. She seemed to be floating on air as the time got closer and closer to the official moment. Timothy just sat back and relaxed. His friend from high school was his best man and Simone was the maid of honor. Everything was in place, except the bride. That was to be expected though.

Andrea watched Timothy sitting there and thought of how much he resembled Bruce. She wished Bruce was there to share in this moment with her. By the way Tim was looking, she was apparently more nervous than he was.

"How are you feeling son?" she asked as she watched him.

"I'm alright Mom, just waiting for this to be over with," he said impatiently.

"Soon enough baby, soon enough. You know I'm going to miss you," she said tearing up.

"Ma, I'm not moving out the state. I'm going to be right across town and you know I'm going to come see you every day," he said standing up to hug her.

"Timothy please don't you worry about your momma. Cleave to your wife fully; I'll be all right. It is my pleasure to watch my child mature into a man that God made. I'm so proud of you son," she said as she cried into his suit jacket.

"Thanks Ma, but I couldn't have gotten here without your prayers, your faith, and your diligence and of course your patience." He bent down and kissed her forehead.

"So are you nervous?" she asked as she pulled a tissue from her purse to blow her nose.

"A little, but I'm ok because this is what I wanted, it's like a dream come through" he said straightening his tie.

"Good, that's how I was with Bruce. I loved that man so much, I wasn't even nervous when our wedding night came," she began reminisce.

"I don't think I'm going to be nervous either," he said with a large grin on his face.

"You so silly boy. Do you know how much you look like Bruce right now?" she said admiring him.

He smiled; he loved every comparison made of him to his dad. He had fond memories of his father, memories that every time they crossed his mind, either laughed or smiled. He remembered how his father looked and especially how he smelled. He used to stand on the toilet and watch his father shave his face and head and when he used to do things around the house. He would watch and mimic his every move. He was his father's shadow, so naturally he took it the hardest when he died. Andrea wasn't the only one wishing he was there to see this day.

"It doesn't hurt anymore you know, I mean his death. But it's times like these that bring back the sting. He'll never get to see my first child and he won't be here to pat me on my back and tell me how beautiful my wife is. It's times like these that made the crack my best friend, now I have God," he said wiping the tears away.

"Baby, your real daddy *is* patting you on your back and he *is* here at your wedding and he *will* see your first born because Bruce was just a steward, your real father is in Heaven." She said, wiping his tears.

"I know but I kinda wish my steward was here too." Just as he said that the Pastor came in. Things had to get started

202

and soon because there was another private ceremony right behind theirs. Timothy ran out the church to see if he had seen Sondra's car parked, it wasn't. He needed to get her here and fast if this was going to happen today. Sondra was lolly gagging with Simone, thank God on the way back to the church.

"So does your mom know yet," Simone asked marveling at the traffic when it's time to go somewhere.

"Heck nah, she would do something stupid to ruin it. Besides, I haven't spoken to her since she tried to be slick and hook me back up with my ex."

"I'm not the one to disrespect any body's mom, but she was stupid for doing that. So when are you going to tell her?" she asked looking at Sondra.

"I'm not sure, I know she's going to have a lot to say but it's not going to matter. I have who I want and that's all that matters to me." Sondra said boldly.

"Let me give you some advice before you get married. I wish somebody would've told me this but it's alright, I know better for next time. Anyway, don't listen to those religious church folk and talk to each other and not at each other. As women, we're so emotional, but find a way to control your emotions and you'll see a situation for what it is, either a mountain or a mole hill. Don't be afraid to ask for help but always go to God first. And last but not least, pray together as much as possible and you pray and keep your relationship strong with God in case his is not."

"Wow thanks Simone, that's the best advice anyone has ever given me. I didn't know you were married," she said now watching Simone.

"Yea, that's why I lived in Germany. My husband was a pilot in the Army and his helicopter malfunctioned and went down off the coast of Greece. They found him months later twelve thousand feet underwater," she said looking out the passenger side window.

"I'm so sorry Simone, I didn't mean to bring that up," Sondra Apologized.

"Bring what up? I don't think about his death, just the life we lived and the love he gave me. He was the best part of my life nothing was more fulfilling. When he died, I couldn't help but to live because I knew he would turn over in his grave if he knew I wanted to die too. That's the type of love I hope you and Tim found. If anything should happen to either one of you, that either of you would live life like it's the both of you" she said as she looked up toward heaven.

"We got that type of love Simone, thanks to God!" she said as she looked down at her phone vibrating. She missed the call but seen it was her soon to be husband. Just as she was about to call him back, Simone's phone rings. The look on her face told her to step on the gas and get to the church in a hurry without getting a ticket or killed.

Sondra pulled up to the church fifteen minutes later, her and Simone jumped out the car in flash. They ran up the stairs of the church where Tim's mother was waiting nervously. Sondra had exactly five minutes to get her dress and shoes on without messing up her hair or makeup while still being thirty minutes late.

The sanctuary had about sixty-five people waiting for the bride as was the groom who was waiting impatiently himself. When he saw his mother enter in, and give him the go ahead nod that signified that his bride was ready, is when the butterflies took flight and felt more like Boeing seven forty sevens in his belly.

As the doors opened, Sondra saw him. He was tall, medium complexion but oh so fine. She walked like a queen down the aisle to the melody the pianist played for her. The pastor fulfilled two roles that day; he walked his friend's daughter down the aisle for him and married her as well. There was no dry eye in the building as Sondra looked like an angel gliding on air. Timothy's eyes were drenched with tears, she was more beautiful than he imagined. As he took his place by her side and said their vows, the tears never stopped. When it came time for the rings, which belonged to his parents, both Tim and Sondra were in tears. The ceremony was a special one for a lot of people. Those that knew Tim and where he came from cried in jubilation for the things the Lord has done.

Sondra was now Mrs. Washington and loved every letter of that name. Let Justine say something now, this time the kid gloves were coming off. After all, she's family now!

# CHAPTER 14

*1 Corinthians 6:9-11 Know ye not that the unrighteous shall not inherit the kingdom of God? Be not deceived: neither fornicators, nor idolaters, nor adulterers, nor effeminate, nor abusers of themselves with mankind, (10) Nor thieves, nor covetous, nor drunkards, nor revilers, nor extortioners, shall inherit the kingdom of God. (11) And such were some of you: but ye are washed, but ye are sanctified, but ye are justified in the name of the Lord Jesus, and by the Spirit of our God.*

The conference was all over but Tyrone was just beginning. Men at every conference threw themselves at him but there was one in particular that he really liked. He was a handsome doctor and so unlike all the others. He was breaking rule number one, never date a single man. Alex was not only single but also he was bisexual and Tyrone knew it. He was everything he wanted and then some. To Tyrone, this wasn't just a simple fling; this was a serious relationship. He was just like Tyrone in so many ways. He dressed wearing the best of everything, smelled good and took exceptional care of his body. Since he was single with no kids, he had the best that money could buy. Tyrone wanted to spend more and more time with Alex but because of his busy schedule, that wasn't possible.

Alex really liked his preacher boyfriend but he wasn't about to take him as serious as he wanted him to. Tyrone had a wife and kids, why would he take him serious? He was just his current toy, a fix for the moment. When he got tired of playing with him, he would put him on the shelf and on to the next one. Tyrone wasn't trying to hear any of that; he wasn't to be played with. He was a man of importance and there was no one that should be before him. At least, that's what he thought of himself.

Latonya Baxter paced the floor of her luxurious bedroom thinking about her husband. She knew he was cheating but not with who. All the signs were there- the late night phone calls, the disappearing acts, he wouldn't touch her and worst of all, he acted as if his own sons didn't exist. Tonya knew she was a catch; she was a good wife and mother. She loved God and kept her family first. When it came to looks she was outstanding. She stood five foot ten inches and weighed about one hundred and forty eight pounds. She was model perfect with a beautiful mocha complexion and beautiful long wavy hair that came from the Italian side of her family.

Her father couldn't stand her husband, he always thought there was something wrong with the man but could never say what. When things started to get rough at home, he made sure to let her know it was time to go. Either she left willingly or he was coming to get her.

"Tonya you and the boys finished packing?" her father asked, driving speedily to Tonya's home.

"Yes we're ready daddy," she answered as she sat down on the bed.

"Good, one of my guys is behind me with the truck to pack all your stuff on. You alright?" he asked noticing her silence.

"I'm fine daddy. I just don't know what to tell the church or our boys," she answered quietly.

"Don't worry about the boys, they know the deal already. Forget about what you're going to tell the church, they don't need to know your business anyway. I'm just glad you're coming home. Your focus should be on those two young men you got. Not that punk that likes to put his hands on you, why didn't you tell me he hit you," he said getting angry.

"Daddy he just pushed me that's all," she said still defending Tyrone.

"I don't care what you call it. My grandsons said he hit you and I believe them. You leave a note for that preacher and tell him I said I got a word from God myself. Tell him I'm coming from the book of Smith & Wesson, the whole forty fourth chapter." He said patting the gun sitting on the seat beside him.

Tonya laughed, as funny as her father sounded she knew he was for real. Tonya hung up with her father and just sat there at the edge of her bed. She may have gotten side tracked but she still remembered how to pray. Tonya just didn't know exactly how powerful her very short prayer would be, but God would answer.

"Lord, reveal the hidden things to me," she prayed.

*Psalms 109:4* *For my love they are my adversaries: but I give myself unto prayer.*

Sondra's mother called the house for the first time in six months. It's been that long since they last spoken. The call went to the answering machine, which was alright since she planned on leaving a message. When the machine came on it said in a male voice, "You've reached Timothy and Sondra, please leave a message with your name and number and we'll return your call at our earliest convenience...beep." She hung up instantly. She assumed they were living together, her daughter and the man she loathed. This was the man that stole her away from her dreams. She called the church and arranged for an emergency meeting with their pastor. Something had to be done.

"Mrs. Ashton, right?" Pastor asked politely.

"It's Ms. Ashton, Pastor," she corrected.

"Oh excuse me Ms. Ashton, how are you today?" he asked as he opened the door for her to his office.

"No disrespect Pastor, but I didn't come here for the small talk, I already know where I can get that. I asked for this meeting to speak of my daughter Sondra" she said crisply.

"Ok, I'm listening," the pastor said as he sat back in his chair.

"She's involved with this creature named Timothy, I don't like him one bit," she said bitterly.

"Do you even know Timothy, Ms. Ashton? Timothy is a great kid and a hard worker, not to mention he puts God first and foremost," the pastor said defensively.

"So you approve of this crack head?" she said incredulously.

"I approve of his testimony," he said as his face frowned in confusion.

"His testimony, how cute, I don't approve of nothing when it comes to him. He stole my daughter away from her dreams," she said in an accusing fashion.

"Was it her dreams or was it yours that he took her away from Ms. Ashton?" he asked knowing the answer.

"I wanted the best for my daughter, he is the absolute worst. I tried to give her prince charming and she chose a pond scum frog instead," she said as she glared at him.

"What makes him the worst? He's a faithful member, a leader, a provider, hard worker and from what I've heard, a great husband," he said as he sat up to meet her glare.

"Husband? He's married and with my daughter?" she asked as she shot to her feet glowering at the pastor. When he realized his mistake, he didn't stand nor said anything further. He let her assume from that point on.

"Oh you don't have to say anything else Pastor. He's gotta go and you just gave me the ammunition to use to make sure that happens. What's happening to our church that a pastor would approve of an adulterer shacking up with his best friend's daughter?" she asked as she threw her weave over her shoulder.

"I trust you remember your way out. It's the same way you came in. Have a blessed day Ms. Ashton," the pastor said in a dismissing fashion. As soon as she walked out of his office and slammed his door, he picked up the phone and called Sondra, no answer. He kept trying to get her and finally she answered. She was at the hairdresser under the dryer when she found out the news. Sondra smiled; it's going to be show down at the OK corral now.

*Hebrews 13:4 Marriage is honourable in all, and the bed undefiled: but whoremongers and adulterers God will judge.*

Sam was head over heels in love with Karen by now. His kids felt the same way and Shawn loved and respected him. He wanted to marry her but she seemed so content with the way things were going. For the first time he wanted to marry again, this was something he thought he would never want to do again after losing his first wife. He wanted to spend the rest of his life with this woman just as he would've spent the rest of his life with his late wife. He knew he was ready for this step, but was she? He gathered the nerves he needed to speak to her and tell her how he felt. It was going to take every single nerve in his body and hers.

"You know Karen, I was thinking that you know every time we kiss things happen in our bodies that sometimes are so strong that they're uncontrollable," he said stalling.

"Sam, where are you going with this? Are you still thinking of what happened between us? Sam we made a mistake, we repented and went to God about it. What else do you want us to do?" she asked, getting frustrated.

"Sex with you was not a mistake Karen, I'm not ashamed to say I enjoyed every minute of it, but umm," he hesitated.

"Ok that's the part I don't like, the but umm part. I'm not pregnant Sam, we have no diseases, and the devil caught us both off guard and weak. So we just have to watch what we do from now on, especially our kisses," she said trying to understand the direction Sam was heading with this conversation.

"That's the thing Karen, I don't want to watch every move we make. I want to kiss you the way I want to kiss and do whatever else as well," he said boldly.

"Ok so you're saying that we should keep having sex? Am I understanding you correctly?" Karen asked, confused for sure now.

"No, what I'm saying is let's get married and do this thing the right way. This isn't satisfying me, I want more Karen," he confessed.

"Oh wow, that much more huh?" she was stunned. Karen had to sit down on that one.

"I know it's a big step and I know you had a rough marriage before. I'm not him and I'm never going to be him. I absolutely love you Karen, you're all that I think of. I can't imagine a day without you. After I lost my wife, I told God

212

that's it; I couldn't and wouldn't be married again. But I never counted on meeting you and now not only has my mind changed, but you've changed my life. You complete me, will you marry me Karen? Please?" he pleaded.

Karen was speechless. All she could do was let the tears go, like she had a choice. She felt loved like she never felt it before. In her heart she felt the same way. She loved Sam more than he could ever know, but was it enough to marry him?

*Ezekiel 25:17 And I will execute great vengeance upon them with furious rebukes; and they shall know that I am the LORD, when I shall lay my vengeance upon them.*

Tyrone came home to an empty house. This wasn't happening, she was supposed to be here through thick and thin, the good and the bad. How could she leave him? Tyrone called her phone, no answer. He called and called and called, still no answer. Tyrone went into a rage, how dare she not answer, did she not realize who he was? Tyrone slapped over lamps, threw vases across the room, and turned over furniture. But when he turned around, it was to see a strange sight. Directly in front of him in the mirror was the reflection of a mad man, sweating profusely with a deep scowl. He didn't even recognize this man as himself at first. This wasn't the handsome, prominent preacher, man of God he proclaimed himself to be. Tyrone stared into his own eyes, what was happening to him?

"Like what you see?" Tonya said, leaning on the doorpost.

Tyrone turned around quickly to see his wife standing there in jeans and a tank top. That wasn't her style.

"I like the new look Tonya," he said as he stared at her, still angry.

"I can't say the same for you, what's going on Ty? Whatever it is, let's fast and pray and we'll get a breakthrough," she said reaching out to him.

"Fast and pray for what? Do you know who I am? I'm going to get my break through regardless of you. I'm not the people I preach to" he said basically spitting in her face.

"Oh my bad Jesus Jr.," she said hurt.

"And don't you forget it wife!" he yelled.

"I don't know what's going on with you but we're not coming back till you're done doing things your way and start doing it the Lords way," she stated plainly.

"Tonya you must've forgotten, you don't add to me, I make you. I don't need you girl, you need me. So take the boys and leave because I'm above only and you're beneath," he said as he dismissed her.

"You're an arrogant backwards jerk. You've gone over the edge and I hope God catches you cause you're not going to enjoy the trip down!" with that Tonya left. Tyrone packed him a bag and went back over to Alex's place. He needed some affection, the kind only Alex could give.

Tonya went to see the Bishop to let him know what was going on. The bishop tried to call Tyrone countless times, but every time he tried to call, Tyrone avoided his calls. Bishop assured Tonya everything would be all right. He would continue to try to reach Tyrone until he answered. Meanwhile, Tyrone was living in sin up to his neck. He wasn't happy though because apparently, he wasn't the only one in Alex's life.

Tyrone walked up on Alex sitting in the living room doing his financial paperwork to open his own practice. He had Alex's phone bill in hand with multiple called numbers circled. He threw the bill on the table in front of him. Once Alex realized what it was, his anger was kindled.

"Who told you that it was alright to go through my mail?" he asked looking up at Tyrone.

"Who do these numbers belong to? Are you cheating on me Alex?" Tyrone asked as he stared at Alex.

Alex rose up from the couch and walked past Tyrone to the kitchen. "I didn't know it was possible to cheat on a married man Ty. Let me tell you something, I'm a grown man. I do what I want and when I want and I don't have to answer any questions concerning it. Oh and understand this, just because we're having sex doesn't mean you own me," he said as he grabbed a bottle of water and put it to his lips.

"You just tried me," Tyrone said as the rage kicked in. Alex wasn't expecting the blow or the ones that followed. Alex was literally knocked out. When he awoke, it was to pain. He quickly got up and looked in the mirror to assess the damage done to his face. His cheek and eye on his right side were swollen shut. His nose and mouth were both bleeding but he didn't think anything was broken. He walked around his condo looking for Tyrone but he and his bags were gone.

Tyrone packed and went home. He surprised himself with the amount of jealousy that was in him. He washed the blood from his knuckles and saw how swollen they truly were. He could barely sleep that night but he didn't call Alex, he wasn't going to call. Tyrone didn't go anywhere for three days. He replayed the incident over and over again in his mind. Finally he called no answer.

Alex had to call in for an entire week in order to let his face heal. It would be one thing to fight and lose, but to be blindsided like that was cowardly and unforgiveable. He saw all the calls and saved all the messages, he wasn't going to answer. Payback might not be physical but Tyrone was going to wish it was when Alex was done with him.

Tyrone was finally back in church. Everyone passed him with broad smiles, women flirting and men wanting to shake his hands. One of the Ushers approached him with orders from the Bishop.

"Evangelist Baxter, Bishop wants to see you right now in his office," he whispered.

"Tell him I'll see him after church," he whispered back.

"Evangelist, he said if you don't come then he'll come out here and get you and you won't like that at all," the usher whispered back. That caused Tyrone to stop and change directions and head to the Bishops office immediately. He knew this was about his marriage and frankly he didn't want to talk about it but to keep his business private, he would entertain the Bishop. He knew that Bishop was a persistent man so there was no time like the present. When they got to the door and the usher opened it, Tyrone froze in his steps. He couldn't move, he couldn't breathe and he dared not look at Bishop and Tonya wouldn't look at him. To his horror, standing at the left side of Bishop was none other than Alex.

"Come in and sit down Evangelist Baxter," Bishop spoke quietly.

"Good morning Bishop, what is this about?" he asked as he took a seat. The usher closed the door silently sealing off the outside world.

"You know this young man to my left quite well don't you Evangelist?" Bishop asked knowingly.

"Yes sir I do," he said not volunteering anything extra.

"Do you know how I know this young man evangelist?" Bishop asked trying to keep his emotions in check.

"No sir I don't," he answered truthfully.

"He's my nephew Tyrone, my dead sister's boy" he said as he could no longer hide his disgust.

Tyrone saw the look creeping up on the Bishop's face and had to loosen his tie. For some reason swallowing was all of a sudden becoming harder for him to do.

"Alex and I had a very interesting conversation about you evangelist. He told me some things that I didn't know. He told me things that shamed me about you Tyrone Baxter. Do you know what those things are boy?" Bishop asked as his anger grew more and more.

Tyrone instantly started to sweat. He looked up at Alex who had a nasty grin on his face. He didn't know just how much he told Bishop but he wasn't going to volunteer any information.

"You put your hands on my kin and not just in a violent way but in an ungodly way. I know all about your abominations boy, how dare you sit here and call me Bishop when you have no respect for Godliness. You might as well call me my first name. You sat right up under me for years, preaching and teaching yet, you were lying to me the whole time. You could've told me the truth and I would've done anything possible that could've helped you, instead, you disgraced yourself, your wife, your whole family, this church and me. You have the audacity to walk boldly into that pulpit knowing that your life is a lie?" Bishop yelled slamming his fist onto the mahogany oak table. He looked like an angry bull. He was standing, leaning over his desk at this point, brows knitted in a frown, nostrils flared wildly as the corners of his mouth turned sharply upward in a brute scowl.

At that point Tonya rose up, turned and looked at her husband. She was standing above him, watching the sweat beads drip down the forehead of this once proud and arrogant world evangelist who now sits looking like a little boy that's about to get the beating of a lifetime.

"I told you, you wasn't going to enjoy the trip down you arrogant bastard. You're not the only one who has to suffer. You're **that** selfish that you wouldn't even consider your own family?" She paused to compose herself before continuing "You put me through hell and for what? A man? I defended you, I loved you and had your children but you'd rather what a man has to offer than what God rightfully gave you. And you were saying **WHO** was beneath Tyrone? I just wanna spit in your face right now, but my spit deserves to land on better trash than you." she said as she walked out.

Tyrone was sweating profusely by this time. His worst nightmare is now his reality. He knew he just lost it all, that quick. All He could do was sit there and shake his head, his wife, his kids, his ministry. All he had worked so hard for, gone. Bishop couldn't take his eyes off of Tyrone; he regarded him as a son. He was so angry he couldn't preach that day. Alex wasn't finished yet. He watched the sweat roll off of Tyrone's temples in anticipation of his next move. "He preached the devil now he's about to meet him." He said as he grinned wickedly.

****ALL SCRIPTURES TAKEN FROM KING JAMES VERSION AND NEW KING JAMES VERSION BIBLE****